MONSTERS

WE'RE ALL A LITTLE DIFFERENT

GLENN ROLFE, TOM DEADY,
AND NICK KOLAKOWSKI

BOOK 5 IN CRYSTAL LAKE'S DARK TIDE SERIES

Let the world know:
#IGotMyCLPBook!

Crystal Lake Publishing
www.CrystalLakePub.com

Join the Crystal Lake community today
on our newsletter and Patreon!

ISBN: 978-1-957133-22-5

Cover art:
Ben Baldwin—http://www.benbaldwin.co.uk

Layout:
Lori Michelle—www.theauthorsalley.com

Edits and Proofs by:
Gregg Feezell, Carson Buckingham, Paula Limbaugh,
Sydney Ngxokela, Karen Runge, and Theresa Derwin

DARK
TIDE

IT CAME FROM THE LAKE

GLENN ROLFE

CHAPTER 1

DEANA COULDN'T BELIEVE Kevin would kill for her. Fifteen years of marriage and she never would have guessed he had it in him—but the blood and brains spilling from Henry Owens' skull, sliding like black mud down the edge of the sheer rock, told her otherwise. Owens—that cheap, adulterous scumbag—would never grope another employee.

She'd tried to let it pass. She'd tried to shake off the subtle touches on her arm, then on her thigh, then the pats on the ass. The full-on molestation of her breast was the straw that snapped the proverbial camel's back. She'd run out crying at the end of that day, and immediately fell into Kevin's arms when he came home from work, where the year and a half of silence amidst Owens' harassment tumbled from her in a wave of sorrow and shame. Now, standing under the dying rays of the summer sun, Kevin dropped the ax to the dark-spotted dirt. He was hyperventilating, but the deed was fucking done. She ran to him and wrapped her arms around his neck.

"You are the greatest man I have ever known."

He was trying to catch his breath. Anxiety had been an enemy of his since he'd hit his mid-thirties. His mother had died from cancer; two weeks later, his father had dropped dead of a heart attack. That sort of shit found its way inside and messed a person up.

"You're gonna be all right," she said, rubbing the back of his neck. "Come with me. Come sit down."

They found a log at the edge of the woods.

Slowly, Kevin's breathing came under control. His hands were still shaking. She grabbed them in hers and brought them to her lips.

"I saw his soul," Kevin whispered. He had yet to look her in the eyes.

"He had it comin', babe," she said.

"I never believed in that shit before," he said. "What if . . . what if God judges me for this?"

In all their time together, not once had Kevin mentioned God. Neither of them came from religion. It never came up in their day-to-day lives. She wasn't sure what to think about it, truthfully.

"If there's a God," she said, "he's seen what that man did. And I know he's done worse to others. *God* knows that son of a bitch had it comin', too."

Kevin raised his chin, looking her in the eyes. "You think so?"

She'd never seen him so weak, so vulnerable—so terrified. She pulled him into her arms. He laid his head on her shoulder and wept. More than he had for either of his parents. His whole body shook with the outburst of emotion.

"Come on, babe," she said, hugging him tighter. "You did real good. We're gonna be fine. You trust me, right?"

"Yeah."

"I'll get him set to go over the edge. You did your part."

"Yeah."

"I'm gonna do it now so we can get home, okay?"

"Okay." He lifted his head, wiped his nose with the bottom of his blood-spattered t-shirt, and ran his forearm across his eyes.

She went to the dead body. The large rock, strapped with chains, waited next to the spot where Owens had fallen. Kevin had done so good. Reaching into her sweatshirt, she pulled the last Master padlock from her pocket and wrapped the free end of the chains around the dead man's ankles. When the makeshift anchor was good, she slapped the arm of the lock through the links and clamped the Master lock shut. From her other pocket, she produced the hemp rope she'd found at a craft store, and tied the corpse's wrists. After loading his pockets with as many rocks as she could fit, she stood and clapped the dirt and the deed from her hands.

She turned toward Kevin. Sweat rolled down the side of her face. She placed her hands on her hips. "Last part, babe. Can you help me?"

Kevin got up and joined her by the rock. He moved as if in a daze, slow and mindless. Deana wondered if she had ruined him. Was it possible? She'd seen what his parents' deaths had done to him. What if this was worse?

She shook the thought away. Kevin would be okay. It might take a while, but he'd be okay.

"If we can get it to the edge, I'll shove it off. If you can lift him and toss him at the same time, he should clear the edge no problem," she said.

Kevin helped her push the rock to the edge. Pebbles sprinkled over from the precipice.

"I got it," she said.

Kevin moved to the body and hefted it up in his arms like a bride.

"On three," she said. "One. Two. Three!"

The rock and the scumbag went over flawlessly. She and Kevin stood holding hands, watching as the small boulder and the dead man splashed into the lake below.

"Let's go," she said.

She gave the kill zone another glance, making sure they hadn't missed anything—a piece of jewelry, a business card, or anything that would tell someone Owens was ever here. It was clear. She stepped over and swiped away the blood droplets in the dirt with her boot. Then she spied the goo on the rock.

"Go start the truck, babe," she said. Kevin's Silverado was parked at the edge of the trail. "I'll take care of this last bit."

"I can wait."

"You've done enough. Go on. I'll be right along."

If she didn't know better, she'd have thought he looked hesitant to enter the woods. He paused for a moment, then clenched his jaw and gave her a nod. His footsteps quickly faded, leaving her with the soundtrack of cicadas and other lovely, tiny, nocturnal critters all ready for the encroaching night. She took off her sweatshirt and used it to bundle up the goop of blood and brain matter that she wasn't about to touch with her boot. The sweatshirt she could burn, but the boots were hundred-and-fifty-dollar Doc Martens. No way were they being sacrificed. With the muck picked up, she scrunched the sweatshirt into a ball and tucked it under her arm. She leaned over the edge and gazed down at the sheet of blackness below. Owens had already sunk.

She started for the woods, and had just stepped past the first tree when she heard the cry. Something primal, yet there was an undeniable human quality to it.

"Kevin?" she called.

She heard a loud thud, and Kevin's muffled groan. Then—silence. Even the cicadas seemed to know when to shut the hell up. The shrill keening came again, echoing a threat that tore through the trees like a sentient thing.

Deana had been to this part of Reagan Forest a million times over the course of her lifetime, but as she scanned the shadowy trees, desperately seeking out the source of that haunted cry, she found it impossible to access the layout of her surroundings in her brain. Terror seized her. She turned and ran in the opposite direction of the truck—away from Kevin, away from whatever creature, human or otherwise, called after her.

Whimpering as she made it back to the sheer cliff and site of the murder she and her husband had just committed, Deana dropped to her knees and stared over the edge. She could jump. She'd seen Tony Label and Duncan Soucy do it dozens of times. One time, Duncan had made the jump right after screwing her. She remembered thinking at the time, *Great, I give it up to the guy and he goes and throws himself off a cliff.* But that was back in the '90s. That was when life was still in front of her. That was when you lived in the moment. When you were young and reckless and too tough to die.

The horrible cry came again, close this time. The thing chasing her down would appear any moment. She knew she wouldn't outrun it through the woods. The nearest dirt road was at least two miles down one of the many paths. And that private road, Lakeside Road, was as dead and desolate as the blacked-out Blockbuster Video building out on Highway 9.

She heard branches snapping as the creature drew near. She stood and faced the woods.

And then, it arrived.

She was not prepared in her darkest of nightmares for the sight of it. Even hunched over as it was, it looked to be at least seven feet tall as it crept toward her. Its slender torso was slightly twisted and covered in thick scales. The long legs ended in flippers. Its hands were webbed, and its head was dark with wet clumps of hair hanging like seaweed braids from its scalp. Two black eyes aimed in her direction. Below them, a half-formed human nose gave way to an awful, teardrop-shaped orifice.

It shrieked and gave chase, first lumbering slow, its large feet *thwapping* against the ground, until it found its stride, galloping toward her.

She smelled the staleness of the lake, the mud and the mire, as the monster wrapped its scaly arms around her and lifted her into the sky. She clenched her eyes shut tight. Free falling, the monster screamed for them both the whole way down.

Moments later, below the surface of the lake, her lungs gave out as she and the beast bumped by the body of Henry Owens. Her last visions were of the creature, and of the man she'd helped kill.

CHAPTER 2

"IS THIS OKAY?" Nick whispered, gently pushing into her. "You okay?"

Leilani reached around and dug her nails into his skinny white ass. "Shut up and just fuck me."

Somewhere between Nick fumbling his dick inside of her and the unnecessary need to make sure she was okay, like she was some delicate fucking tulip, loud voices had broken out outside his bedroom. The door burst open. Nick flopped out of her and threw himself against the wall next to the bed. Leilani covered herself with the comforter.

"What the hell do you think you're doing?"

It was Todd, Leilani's foster father. Beside him stood Tina, her foster mom.

"Honey, let me," the woman said, holding Todd back and ushering him away into the hallway. Tina turned her attention to the teenagers in the bed. "Jesus, Leilani. This is how you repay our trust?" Tina walked to where Leilani's jeans lay on the floor and tossed them along with Leilani's underwear to the bed.

Leilani caught the clothes and followed her foster mom's gaze to Nick's bowl, and felt the furthering judgement before Tina opened her mouth again.

"Wait, are you . . . are you high?"

It was no use arguing with them. Not here. Leilani kicked the comforter off and pulled her underwear on. As she stood and stepped into her jeans, she couldn't hold back. "How did you know I was here?"

Arms folded across her chest, her beautiful blue eyes suddenly mean, Tina said, “Does it matter?”

Leilani’s gaze moved from Nick’s bowl to the shiny new iPhone. “Oh my God, did you and Todd track me with my phone?”

“Finding you like *this*, I’d say we did the right thing.”

“Oh yeah, I’m being such a bad girl. I’m not fucking stoned on Oxi or robbing liquor stores—”

“Leilani, that’s enough. Get out to the car. Right. Now.”

“Sorry, Nick.”

Tina stepped past Leilani and stared down the skinny, shaggy-haired boy. “Do your parents know what you’ve been up to?”

“They—they know I smoke.”

Tina threw her hands up. “What a world.”

“Well,” Nick dared. “At least my parents are cool and honest about it. And I’m not out doing worse things behind their backs.”

Tina pointed at him, but couldn’t come up with a retort.

Leilani gave Nick a quick smile from behind her foster mom’s back. “Can we just go before he never wants to hang out with me again?”

“We’ll discuss that at home.”

Tina led Leilani out of the room. Leilani made a kissy face at Nick, who smiled in return and gave a weak wave as she left.

The car ride home was of brutal silence. Impending doom replaced every particle of oxygen. Leilani wanted to hate them right now, but there was a bit of guilt and, even though she loathed it, shame sprinkled over her *furrowed brow* and her *arms-crossed* attitude. She knew they were going to hit her with the whopper of them all. Tina and Todd weren’t like her past foster parents. They wouldn’t strike her or treat her like trash. No, they were going to lower the big fat hammer of justice: *We’re disappointed. Dun-dun-dunnn!*

Leilani wasn’t used to fucking up and giving a shit. This was new territory. And she didn’t like it.

Todd stroked his graying goatee. His brown eyes cast a heavy gaze her way.

Leilani wished she could just melt into a puddle under the table. The anticipation was fucking killing her. “Just punish me already,” she whined.

Tina sat down beside Todd. Her bleach-blonde hair pulled back in a ponytail, her nose ring and the tattoos that sleeved her right arm spoke of someone who used to be cool and should be totally understanding in a situation such as this—but as she began her rhetoric, Leilani knew you couldn't judge a zebra by its stripes.

"You understand we're here to watch out for you and to help keep you safe, right?"

"Yes." She said it, but Leilani wasn't one hundred percent sure she believed anyone in this shitty world wanted what was truly best for her.

"We know," Todd started, "that you've been through some tough places and situations nobody, especially a young person, should have to go through. Life hasn't been fair to you. But . . . .and I say this with my heart . . . we need you to be able to trust us. And likewise, we need to be able to trust you."

Leilani clenched her fists under the table. *Easier said than done.*

Todd continued. "We're going to need you to prove that you can be trusted. Part of our job is to prove to you that we care. You're going to have to meet us halfway."

"And part of our showing you that we care," Tina added, "is teaching you that your actions have consequences."

Leilani knew something was coming.

Tina reached her hand across the table. "I need your phone."

"What? Why? You guys just got it for me."

"And now you've lost that privilege for the next two weeks."

"What? That's bullshit." But she took the phone from her pants pocket and slid it across the table.

Tina handed it to Todd. He put it in his shirt pocket. "You're also grounded for those two weeks," he said. "No going out except to school or with one of us to the store."

"You can't do that. I just made friends here. If you have my phone and I can't go see them . . . that's not fair."

Todd stood. "If you want to get out, you can fill out some job applications online. If you get a job, you can go to school and work."

"Listen," Tina said. "I know this seems harsh, but I don't think it's unfair. We caught you smoking weed and having sex. Those were your choices. Your actions. These are the consequences."

Leilani stood, tears filling her eyes. She wanted to scream. She wanted to grab one of the goddamn table chairs and throw it across the room. Instead, she turned and started toward her room.

"Nick was right, you know. What we were doing isn't anything terrible these days."

"Two weeks," Todd said. "Then we can discuss expectations and what is and isn't acceptable."

"Arrrghh." Leilani left the kitchen and went down the hall. She slammed the bedroom door as hard as she could.

She flopped down on her bed and buried her face in her arms. She cried until she fell asleep.

Later that night, after her foster parents had gone to bed, Leilani dumped her school shit out of her backpack and onto the bed, packed a few sets of clean clothes, a lighter, her own glass bowl and the small Ziplock baggie of weed Nick had given her, and the two hundred and thirty-four dollars she'd managed to squirrel away from babysitting Isla Nutting, the little girl next door. She'd made much more, but she'd spent it on dumb shit. The last thing she nabbed was her ancient iPod. It was a gift from a kid at her last school. They'd made out, nothing more than that. She'd heard he'd since got himself in trouble beating the snot out of his mother, but that didn't make sense. He'd never seemed angry or threatening in the least bit while she'd known him. She would have thought the story was fabricated garbage had she not seen it on the news for herself. It was tragic.

Leilani tucked her earbuds and the music player in the front pocket, and grabbed the comforter and pillow from her bed. Using rope from the junk drawer in the kitchen, she rolled the blanket around the pillow to carry it more easily. Her cell phone sat on the kitchen countertop—staring at her, daring her. For a moment, she thought of what her disappearance might do to Todd and Tina. For a moment, she second guessed this shitty move. Their spying on her and tracking her was a fucking violation of her privacy and proved that they didn't trust her. They wanted to see her be a bastard child. She'd show them what a piece of shit kid was really like. Maybe they'd take her back, maybe not. Fuck it. They were just setting her up for heartbreak anyway. They'd get sick of her and regret bringing her into their home soon enough, and she'd just end up back in the system.

Wiping the tear from the corner of her eye, Leilani returned to her room, zipped up her sweatshirt, grabbed a knit cap, and shouldered her bag, tossing the rolled-up blanket and pillow across her shoulders.

The night was cool as she climbed out her second-floor window, her boots finding the ground below. The buses in Portsmouth were done for the night, but she'd crash nearby and catch the first one in the morning. She didn't plan on going too far; she just needed someplace to lay low for a few days. It was a shitty move, but she was a shitty person.

Easy come, easy go.

From the sidewalk, she glanced over her shoulder and took in the Cruz house. They deserved less of a burden.

Leilani stuffed her thumbs under her bag's shoulder straps and started off into the quiet night.

CHAPTER 3

KRISTIN DEBAUN-OWENS sat behind the large oak desk in her missing husband's office. Her long black hair was pulled back, with two free strands framing a pretty face that hid its fair share of secrets. Dressed in a tight-fitting black dress and smoking a cigarette, she'd had some work done, that was for sure—fake tits, and those ridiculous Botox lips, probably some cosmetic eyebrow shit—but she looked good. She reminded him of that woman from *Friends*; the one who'd starred in those '90s horror movies with the ghostface killer. She looked a hell of a lot better than some of the plastic bitches he'd worked for in the bigger cities.

Maddox sat across from her, watching a thousand possibilities for her husband's sudden disappearance scroll through her mind. This wasn't the first time Henry Owens had run off unannounced. Maddox was well versed in the Owens couple and their 'quiet' affairs. The Owens Company prided itself on its stability as a corporation in the public eye. In the eleven years of the couple's marriage, despite themselves, the company had faced zero scandals. Henry's penchant for vanishing as if he were some big deal magician had created trickier situations as of late. It was obvious that the missus here despised it when things went beyond her control.

"I want to thank you ahead of time for your discretion in this matter, Mr. Maddox."

He nodded and reached across the desk for the envelope.

"Not so fast," she pulled the money back. "You report every bit of minutia back to me. Every. Bit. I don't care how insignificant it may seem to you; I want to know it all. My husband has a history of being peculiar. Anything could be a hint, a clue to what he's been doing or where he might have gone. Are we clear?"

"It appears so," Maddox said.

She pushed the envelope toward him. He picked it up and tucked it away in the inside pocket of his coat.

"Aren't you going to count it?" she asked.

He stood and walked to the door. "If it's not all there, I know where to find you."

Maddox tossed the envelope to the passenger seat of his Toyota and lit an American Spirit. He sat back, waiting for Mrs. DeBaun-Owens to exit the building. He trusted no one, least of all rich people. They were the biggest liars. He had learned long ago to keep tabs on his employers. Was it good business? He didn't care. It was his business, and he wasn't into being fucked over. Plus, if he happened to scrounge up a little dirt on them, he could always leverage it to his advantage.

It was a good twenty minutes before she came outside. A valet brought her black SUV to the curb and opened the door for her. Maddox took a drag of his cigarette and watched as she traced a finger down the young man's jawline before getting into the gas-guzzling vehicle and driving off. He tossed his butt out the window, and pulled out into the avenue.

CHAPTER 4

ON CLEAR MORNINGS like this, he could still hear the ghosts of the boys left behind. Some cried for their mothers or wives, others could do nothing but sputter nonsense as they gurgled up their life force. Gunfire, scattered *blatts* and the barrage of bullets whizzing by your ears, the *thup-thup-thup* of tree bark or dirt getting pelted as Charlie opened fire from unseen spaces and shadows in the forest ahead.

For Francis Owens, the war was never far from his thoughts. Fifty years on and the nightmares were only now beginning to fade at the edges. Some days were better. He could sit out here on the steps and not hear anything but nature. Henry said he should have remarried. No sense in living out here alone—but after the deaths of Agatha, his wife of thirty-two years, and their only child, Gertie, Francis hadn't found the heart or the will to replace them. There simply *was* no replacing them.

Tears no longer came at their memory. He'd dried up ten years back.

On his good days, Francis could find something in those old files in his head to smile about, a silly thing one of them had done at some point to make him laugh. Days like this, though, there was no laughter, were no smiles . . . the sunshine didn't reach his soul. If it could, he was certain it would only burn. He wasn't a monster, no—vampires and werewolves were for movies. He was a breathing ghost of sorts, unable to be truly free of his past—but here he was, taking in air just the same.

He gripped his walking stick and with a few pops and groans, he stood and looked into the trees. There was no VC out there. Most of his brain knew that, but he heard them anyways.

He wasn't alone here. Despite what his brother believed. It wasn't just the specters of his past that roamed the lake region, either. Francis was a caretaker. His charge kept its distance. It was best for them both. He still needed to get out there and get rid of the Chevy. He'd been lazy. Getting old sucked, but sooner or later that kind of slip would bring the outside world to his doorstep. He didn't need that. Not with all the secrets buried around this lake.

Today—yes, *today*—he would clean up the mess over near the inlet road. It had already been a week. Luck was about done with him. Best not to push it any further.

As he started back toward the steps, Francis heard Creedence Clearwater Revival telling him to run through the jungle. He heard the far away sound of chopper blades, and the whimpering of Tommy Murphy. Eighteen and dying, his insides strewn over his crotch and spilling into the mud beneath him.

It was a bad day. The ghosts were going to be fucking with him until he went to bed. But there was clean up to be done. He'd just have to push on through and hope it wasn't one of the *really* bad days. Even as the thought drifted through his mind like an apparition in the fog, his good hand began to shake. The tremors accompanied the harder days. He wasn't sure the reason, but the correlation was undeniable.

Catching a shadow out of the corner of his eye, he spun.

There's nothing there.

The mental statement became an instant lie on a conspiratorial level. It was not to be trusted. Someone was out here all right. Francis backed up a few steps, making sure to keep the shaded area beneath the canopy of trees in front of him. Charlie hadn't gotten him yet.

There's no one out here.

"Shut up," he said in a hushed voice. "Christ, they'll hear you. You'll get us all killed."

Before he could reassure himself that it was all in his head, Francis hurried into the cabin, grabbed his pistol from beneath his pillow, and wandered back outside to wait. There was something on the wind today. It reminded him of death.

He would sit here and wait.

Wait.

CHAPTER 5

LEILANI GOT OFF the Greyhound in Augusta, Maine, and wandered away from the bus station. She'd been to Maine once before. It was pretty much like most of New Hampshire—the whitest place in America. Her light cocoa skin and Samoan heritage had her sticking out like a sore thumb up here. Her birth parents were from Hawaii, and how she'd ended up in the northeast was as much a mystery to her as the names of the two shitheads who gave her away. She kept her kinky-curly black hair pulled back in a ponytail ninety percent of the time. She caught the odd shitty slur from a moron here or there, but usually it was just lowbrow rednecks giving her nasty looks. She was used to the silent judgement. She didn't really give a fuck anymore.

Augusta was small for a capital city. The main shopping area was a Walmart surrounded by other big-name stores. Ulta Beauty, Eddie Bauer, Old Navy, Barnes and Noble, a Regal cinema, plus restaurants like Panera Bread, Chipotle, and Elevation Burger. She didn't have much money, so Walmart would have to do. She made her way down the busy stretch of road. No one slowed or stopped, and she had yet to see any cops. Augusta was probably used to seeing teenage girls out meandering in the middle of the day. There were a couple of small colleges nearby, too. Maybe she passed for eighteen.

Fall was here, but summer's warmth was clinging to its final days. Had it not been for the stupid wind and clouds, this would've been a hot and sweaty October morning. The grayness was just fucking depressing, and she didn't need anything else bringing her down. She shoved the thoughts of Todd and Tina from her mind, and focused on the task at hand.

By the time she walked through the Walmart doors, she had her shopping list figured out and her pennies spent down to the very last one. Without knowing how long she'd be in the area, Leilani thought it best to load up on nuts and granola, the cheapest filtration set up she could find for water, a tarp to keep dry, and anything that would keep her warm at night. The plan was to camp out in the woods on the edge of town. Her friend, Kyra, had mentioned once how pretty the next town over was. Belgrade was supposedly covered with woods and lakes. It sounded like the perfect hideaway.

Once she had all she could carry, Leilani exited Walmart and the Augusta Marketplace, and headed back the way she came. She considered hitchhiking, but after seeing the leering eyes of the first creep who slowed down, she decided to suck it up and march her way out of town.

I should have bought a knife.

The walk was way longer than she would've thought, especially carrying her loaded backpack and shopping bags. Two cars had pulled up and offered her a ride, but she declined. Better safe than sorry. As she passed the ***Welcome to Belgrade*** sign, sweating like a two-hundred-pound man, she stepped off the side of the road and walked into the trees, ready to park her ass at the first clearing she could find.

The trees were thick here. Nature was still in control in these parts. She could plant herself between a few of the thicker tree trunks, but it would be a little tight. She gazed over her shoulder. Vehicles whizzed by on the other side of trees separating her from the main route and the forest beyond. Not wanting to be too close to the main road, Leilani ventured deeper.

There could be wild animals around. Surely there'd be foxes and racoons, probably some bunnies and deer. She wasn't sure about mountain lions and bears. Did they have those in this part of Maine? She'd sleep easier believing not. She didn't have a gun—not that she'd even know how to use one. *Point and squeeze the trigger*, her mind told her.

Yeah, things always sound easy in your head.

Like running away because you got caught doing something stupid.

It wasn't stupid. It was normal.

Leilani smirked and shook her head. Done arguing with herself, she knelt and shed the bag from her shoulders. Pulling out the mp3 player and headphones from the zippered side pocket, she sunk the ear buds in place and turned on the device. After a minute, a menu screen popped up. She used the down arrow on the thumb pad, scrolling through a bevy of playlists she'd made. Her scrolling stopped on one—*Nick's Picks*. In her huff to get the hell out of Todd and Tina's, she hadn't thought about him. They weren't in love, or anything. It wasn't like that. Was it?

No.

Jesus, I hope not.

Even as the thought wormed its way through her chest and down into her stomach, a yearning begged to differ. Leilani hit the play button, and regretted it.

The soft acoustic guitar and keyboard intro of *Ours* by Taylor Swift filled her head.

She swallowed hard.

You are a real asshole.

I know.

Leilani wiped the wetness from her blurring eyes and pushed on.

After ten or fifteen minutes, the trees thinned. Stepping from the trees, Leilani found the most breathtaking vision she'd seen since a shirtless Thor first crossed her TV screen. It was a lake, resting here in the comfort of complete silence. She dropped her pack to the ground behind her and sat on some rocks at the water's edge. She tucked her knees up to her chest and clasped her fingers together around them. She gazed out over the water and just breathed. Her eyes welled up, and the tears seeped free. Alone again and surrounded in serenity, she let herself cry. Being a teenager was fucking shitty. Being an orphaned teen bumped from one horrible family to the next was even shittier. Running from the best situation you'd landed in in a very, very long time . . . well, that was just being a selfish brat. And for the first time in a while, Leilani felt like *she* was the shithead trying to ruin her life.

She wiped her face dry, shouldered her backpack, and started making her way around the lake. Part of her hoped she'd find a summertime cabin left on its own for the season. There had to be lots of rich fuckers who only occupied this area under the summer sun.

The first place she came upon was at the end of a roped-off section of dirt road. ***No Trespassing*** signs littered the trees like the flyers for indie rock bands she'd seen stapled to telephone poles back in downtown Portsmouth. Figures she'd find the one place owned by the county loony-toon. There was probably some grizzled old recluse or raggedy witch back here waiting for a dumb kid to come stumbling upon the shack in the woods to be eaten alive.

The cabin came into sight.

A snapping branch behind her caused Leilani's skin to tighten and gooseflesh to spread across the backs of her arms.

CHAPTER 6

QUINCY WONDERED WHEN he was going to get caught. Would he get caught? Living with his dad since the start of this past summer, he'd decided at some point that he didn't care about school. He'd skipped a day a week so far since things had started back up at the end of August. Being a freshman sucked. The jock asshole upperclassmen had lived up to their prickish reputations. Aside from his friend, Harvey, Quincy didn't really hang around with anyone. People kind of annoyed him. He preferred animals, nature, and science. His dad worked at a shipbuilding place called Bath Iron Works. He went in before it was light out, and always came home late after going out with his buddies. It made things easier for Quincy to come and go and do as he pleased, including skipping school to hang out at his sanctuary in the woods. The offseason cabin he'd claimed as his own sat on the man-made lake in the woods. Though not all the places out here were empty. Francis Owens—brother to that rich creep, Henry Owens, who owned half of Augusta and this particular lake area here in Belgrade—lurked around the area keeping an eye on things and making sure no drunk teenagers were messing with anything. Quincy had had to hide from the old coot several times in the last two weeks alone. Francis was a wildcard. The old man didn't look like much, but the stories of his outbursts often wove through the rumor mills at school. One kid said Francis had murdered his own wife and son and gotten away with it. Quincy wasn't sure what was true, but believed in playing it safe over the alternative.

He reached the two-level cabin, and did a quick sweep of the perimeter to be sure Francis wasn't nearby. With the coast clear, he opened the unlocked window at the side of the building, tossed his backpack through, and hefted himself inside. The place smelled of pine needles and wood. He loved it. He walked through what would serve as the dining area, the floor creaking with each step, and spoke aloud as he entered one of the now-bare bedrooms.

"Come out, Jester."

Locating his cabin buddy, Jester—a squirrel who'd made his hideout here, too—Quincy watched his furry pal gnawing an acorn in the corner of the room. Jester continued with his nut, unfazed by Quincy's appearance in the room.

"I think I'm gonna head to the lake today. You want to come?"

Jester continued to ignore him.

"Suit yourself."

He had been thinking about the lake a lot lately. No one was allowed to swim, fish, or boat on it besides Francis. He wondered what the point of making something was if no one could use it. He'd almost gone swimming a few weeks ago before the nights started to cool down, but didn't get beyond dipping his feet in the water.

As with Francis, the lake itself had strange stories attached to it. The placid body of water was filled with leeches that would latch to your skin and suck your blood until they popped like oblong, crimson grape tomatoes. Deformed fish missing eyes and fins, or ones with too many eyes and a taste for the flesh of children. Quincy had nightmares about those ones. The creepiest legend revolved around a lake monster that walked upright like a man, called the 'Nietzsche Anathema'. Harvey's older brother, Thomas, freaked him out with tales of the monster kidnapping beautiful women and drowning them before taking them down to some cave-like opening at the bottom of the lake. When Quincy tried to talk to his dad and his dad's girlfriend about the lake monster, they laughed at him and told him to go find it, kill it, and bring them its head. They were also usually smoking weed, so he just took his questions someplace where they wouldn't ridicule him.

One Saturday last month, his dad dropped him off in Augusta at the Maine State Public Library. It was there, in an old book called *Maine Ghost Stories and Folklore*, that he found the creature's name. 'Nietzsche' was a Socrates-type guy who had written a famous line about staring into the abyss and it staring back. 'Anathema' was a prayer or curse. The artificial body of water was said to have been made extremely deep at its center. According to the book, the person who owned the land before the Owens family purchased it had placed a curse on the newly made lake. The Nietzsche Anathema was that curse. That angry individual was unknown; the book had nothing else on them or their family.

Quincy dreamt once about his mom coming to visit him, but in the dream, she never made it to his house. Her Toyota was found abandoned down by the lake, her favorite coat, a green leather jacket, floated just out of reach from the muddy banks. The memory of the dream was shattered when a shriek from deep in the woods stole his breath. Quincy's heart hammered in his small chest like thousands of miniature angry villagers at the gates, demanding the head of their coward king.

CHAPTER 7

WHAT MADDOX WAS able to ascertain about the Owens couple in less than twenty-four hours was astounding. These two were lucky they had so much fucking clout. Their affairs weren't exactly hidden. He had found several 'companionship' searches on Henry Owens' laptop, which he'd acquired from the apartment the man kept separate from the large estate he shared with the missus. The apartment was located in a newly constructed building in a shithole city called Waterville. Henry preferred local girls. The cheaper the better. The bastard no doubt had a list of perversions he liked to perform with his desperate employees, as well. There were files on several thumb drives that Maddox hadn't yet decided whether he needed to open.

Owens was the epitome of the American Dream and all that came along with it. From the local celebrity, to the philanthropist handing out cash to conniving sycophants because he didn't know any better, to the power-corrupted lying piece of shit who was now missing in action. He could be dead, or off on an unannounced getaway with one of his honeys in Florida as the missus thought, or sleeping off a drug-induced sexcapade in some shitty motel outside of town. Outside of providing evidence that Owens was every bit the caricature Maddox assumed him to be, the apartment and laptop were a dead end.

When he returned to the office building, choosing to park on a nondescript backstreet, Maddox puffed on a cigarette as he sat on a curb just down the street, and he phoned Ms. DeBaun-Owens.

"I expect you found him," she said.

"Not quite, but you may want to see this. Come alone. 324 Main Street. Waterville."

"Surely you don't think I'm risking being seen out now?"

"You want to know what your husband's doing right now? Meet me at the address. Twenty-five minutes. You don't show thirty minutes from now, we're done, and I'm gone."

"Listen, *I'm* paying *you*. I tell you what to—"

"324 Main Street. Be there or don't. It doesn't fucking matter to me."

He hit end on the call before finishing his cigarette and tossing it to the dirt behind the bench. Less than five minutes later, she was out of the building, into her SUV, and squealing away.

Perfect.

Entering the side door she'd ordered him to use the day before, Maddox made his way to the small café on the second floor. He scanned the cast of characters for someone who might have the information he was looking for. Two women, maybe early fifties, chatted away at the coffee machine. A younger man with a patchy beard and skinny jeans scrolled through his phone at the nearest table. But the woman sitting alone–hand to her mouth as she gazed at the little smartphone screen before her, her forehead creased above watery eyes–was the one who caught his attention.

Maddox made his way to the cooler and chose an overpriced bottle of Fiji water. He paid the clerk and made his way to the table with the concerned woman.

"Sorry," he said. "Mind if I have a seat?"

Her gaze moved from him to the other empty tables in the room. He could tell she was wondering why didn't just grab his own, but also that she didn't have the fight at the moment to tell him no.

"Sure."

"Thanks," he said, pulling out a chair and sitting down to swig from his drink. "I don't mean to pry, but I'm here for a visit with Mrs. DeBaun-Owens. And truthfully, she kind of scares me."

The creases above her brows eased at this. Her eyes almost smiling. "Yeah, she's something. What are you seeing her about?"

"Possible job opportunity. I'm a pretty good PR man."

The woman rolled her eyes. "Good luck with that. She's got quite the team already."

"Thanks. Say, are you alright?"

She looked his way.

"Sorry, you just looked . . . concerned."

"It's probably nothing," she said, looking back to the phone in her hands.

"Well, anything to help take my mind off my interview for a few minutes would be nice. Is it something bad?"

"My friend Deana, she works here, mostly with Mr. Owens . . . well, she left Friday after work, and nobody's heard from her or her husband since."

"Oh, sorry. I'm sure they're okay. I mean, it's Maine. What could have happened to them, really?"

"I don't know," she said. She glanced around the room before turning her attention back to him. When she spoke again, her voice was just above a whisper. "Mr. Owens is AWOL, too."

Maddox leaned forward and lowered his voice to match hers. "Doesn't he take business trips?"

"Yeah, I suppose, but . . . Deana told me—oh, I shouldn't say anything. You're here for an interview. I don't want to start you on gossip before you even have a chair in the room."

"Hey, if the salary is close to what I was led to believe, I'm not turning down any offer they want to extend to me."

"If you're sure . . . well, Deana's a decent-looking girl, ya know. But she's married. Has been with Kevin since high school. She told me Mr. Owens has a thing for her. No surprise, he's a gross hound dog, but Deana thwarted his advances and she said he's been mad at her since. She said he . . . " lowering her voice further still, the woman spilled. "She said he even grabbed her ass last week. I told her she should report him or quit. She shouldn't have to put up with that sort of behavior."

"Sounds awful."

"I shouldn't say anything. It's just . . . it's just her and Kevin are both missing and so is Mr. Owens. It's odd is all."

"Coincidence, I'm sure of it. They'll all show up. When did you last see her?"

"Friday afternoon. We walked to our cars together. I asked her if she wanted to go grab a few drinks, but she seemed off, like she had something heavy on her mind. She said she had plans at the lake."

"The lake?"

"It was weird."

"What's weird?"

"Mr. Owens owns the lake."

After watching the woman whose name he never got exit the café, Maddox was up and heading down the hallway, and racing back out to his car. Once behind the wheel, he did a search for Owens and his lake and found the location. It seemed like he might be in town a little longer than anticipated. He'd find some accommodations on the water. When his gut felt this sure about something, he knew his instincts were always right. Another quick search pulled up the newly restored Megill House. A bed and breakfast around Long Lake. He normally used generic motels, ones where you could easily blend in, free to roam in and out like the invisible man, but a good bed and breakfast could offer local color and stories about the uppity business assholes who came in and muddled things up for small-town folk.

CHAPTER 8

BRIAN CUMMINGS HATED his ex-girlfriend's new man, Jake. The guy was a legit douchebag narcissist. What kind of grown man took a thousand selfies and littered Instagram with them like he was some kind of model-slash-rock star? A jerk, that's who. It'd be slightly more acceptable if the tool was an actual influencer on social media, but he wasn't. He was just a self-centered assclown. Fuck him. And worst of all, Heather was head over heels for the guy. It was enough to make Brian want to barf.

An orange triangle symbol lit up on the dashboard of his Subaru. Fuck if he knew what the symbol meant. He was trying to recall the exact warning when a loud pop exploded somewhere beneath the car. The steering suddenly pulled hard to the right.

"Fucking bullshit."

Brian wrestled with the wheel to get the shaking vehicle out of the road. He glanced at the rearview, and was grateful no one had been behind him. He hung his head, took a deep breath, and killed the engine before shoving the door open and climbing out of the car.

Somehow, this was that loser Jake's fault. It wasn't relevant, but Brian had been thinking of the guy when the tire blew, so ipso facto, yeah, Brian would blame it on the man who had become the bane of his existence. His first thought was to call Heather and tell her, but she'd posted this morning on Facebook about her excitement over Jake meeting her at work to take her out to lunch. The guy was getting on Brian's last fucking nerve.

Stepping from his Subaru, he caught the glimmer of Owens' Lake. He'd heard some pretty far-fetched tales about the area. Lake monsters, crazy toxic fish. It was so stupid. People could be duped into believing anything. Like Heather with this Jake character.

Brian had just pulled the spare and tire jack from the trunk when a scream exploded from the woods to his right. Goosebumps broke out along his arms.

Do foxes cry like humans?

He'd heard a YouTube clip of one, once. It was terrifying.

It's not a person.

But it sounds like one . . .

He waited to hear if the cry would come again. When nothing happened, he set to work on changing the blown tire. He didn't know much about fixing cars, but he could change a damn tire. Plus, maybe it would be therapeutic to wrench on something for a few minutes.

He and Heather had had some bad fights the last year of their relationship, but nothing he'd thought would end things. He'd been wrong. According to Heather, she'd been checked out of the romance for at least the last year. Apparently she thought of him as a friend, almost a brother.

He'd just finished tightening the last nut—imagining it were a wire around Jake's throat—when the cry came again. Brian wasn't the type of guy spoiling for a fight, he wasn't even what some would consider brave, but he did care about the general wellbeing and safety of others—ex-girlfriends' new boyfriends excluded.

Gripping the tire iron in his hand, he entered the woods and walked in the direction of the scream. Another shriek exploded, and he simultaneously froze and tried to run. The urge to act won out as he raced through the trees, the low brush and webbed branches lashing him as he crashed through them; his forty licks of penance for all that unwarranted hatred of Heather's new boyfriend. A little ways in, as he closed in on the lake, a cabin came into view. He was about to step from the trees onto the dirt path leading to the quiet home, when the scent of something dank and rotten hit his nostrils and clung there, like a mucus set on suffocating him. His gag reflex worked as he tried to hold down the flatbread breakfast pizza he'd eaten an hour ago. There was no time to look for the source. He turned and found himself in the shadow of a grotesque impossibility.

Piss poured down the inside of his khakis. Trembling to his core, Brian's mouth dried to the point he was sure it could tear at any given moment.

The towering beast man-thing standing before him threw its

large, webbed hands around Brian's face and yanked him forward, clamping its weird suction cup orifice over Brian's mouth and nose. A gush of putrid water flooded past Brian's teeth, washed over his tongue and forced its way down his throat. He wanted to gag and expel out whatever funk this thing was imparting upon him, but already he couldn't feel his body or even breathe. Shock walloped him—and the creature did the rest. Wrapped in the obscenity's scaly arms, still in a lip-lock that kept him from moving, Brian was pulled along from the trail, his brand-new leather Aviator shoes catching every root and rock along the way to the waiting waters beyond. He was seven years old again, lying on the couch cushions he'd lined up on the floor next to his mother's side of the bed, crying because nightmares of the movie *The Birds* wouldn't allow him to sleep. His dad snoring like a dying chainsaw somewhere on the bed above; Jay Leno on the 13-inch television screen, volume so low Brian could barely make out his weird voice. And the night strangely out of sync, oddly uneven—like a black and white episode of *The Twilight Zone* where nothing was quite as it seemed. Brian was all the way back there again in the darkened room, swallowed in the TV light as the tears spilled down his cheeks. Blood and bile dribbled from the corners of his mouth where the creature's lips didn't quite reach. His last thought was how funny it was that he no longer cared about Heather or Jack. There were only the final brainwaves carrying fear.

The last of his air gone from his lungs, Brian went into convulsions as the mythical lake monster took him under.

CHAPTER 9

LEILANI AWOKE IN a dim room filled with shadows and the scent of wet earth. A throbbing in the back of her head reminded her of the attack. She'd been staring at the side of a cabin at the end of the dirt path when a branch snapped behind her. Something hard slammed into the back of her skull.

She was inside the cabin. A shuffling sound somewhere to her right froze her in place, the thrumming in her head slowing her reflexes. She watched as a man emerged through the cloud of dust motes floating between her place on the floor and the window behind him. A raspy voice spoke.

"Don't worry. I ain't tryin' to keep ya here. And I ain't no peddo or kiddie fiddler. So don't worry."

Leilani reached for the wet spot at the back of her skull. Her fingers came back bloody.

"Didn't mean to catch you with that pole, neither. You startled the hell out of me, young lady. I just about flipped out of my skin at the sight of ya."

Accidently hit her with a pole? *As-fucking-if.* Leilani scanned the room. The door to the outside world was just off to the right. Normally, she'd be able to reach that distance way before this old recluse could make a grab for her—but there was no telling if her legs would carry her, or spill her to the wooden floor. She knew she probably had a concussion. She'd have to try and stand to be sure.

"Let me get you some water."

The man was hefting a thick piece of birch as a walking stick. She watched him make his way to the sink across the room. He had no noticeable limp, no handicap she could ascertain from his gait. While he had his slightly humped back to her, she rose from the couch and felt the world slide to the side like she'd just risen from her seat at the Mad Hatter's table. Her stomach tumbled as her balance reeled, and without warning she threw up.

"Huh?" the old man turned from the running faucet, the glass of water in his hand. "Girl, what are ya doin'? Sit down for Christ's sake."

She wiped her chin as she flopped back down onto the couch. "I'm sorry. I didn't mean to—"

"Don't worry about that." He made his way across the room and handed her the glass of water. "I've dealt with far worse than a little vomit."

The glass was cold and felt good in her hands. She sipped it, careful not to trigger another revolt in her guts. "Thank you."

He came back and dropped a ratty hand towel over the small puddle she'd purged. "Name's Francis. You got one?"

"Um, yeah. Leilani."

"What's that? South Pacific?"

"It's Hawaiian."

"Huh? You're a long way from home, ain't ya?"

"I've never really been there?"

"How come? Your parents from here?"

"No—I mean, I'm not sure."

"You're not sure?"

"Do you have a phone I can use?"

She didn't really have anyone to call, but she didn't want to answer any more questions about where she came from. Not to this guy. Not to anyone.

"You're out here traipsin' 'round my house, that lake. It ain't safe out here, ya know." Francis' gaze went blank. Whatever he was looking at, it wasn't here in this room with them. After a few more seconds, he returned. "Shouldn't you be in school?"

She didn't want to reveal anything else to this man, especially since he didn't seem quite right. She hadn't decided if he was a threat or not. Better to play it safe and keep what she could as a buffer between them. God, she didn't want to stay here any longer than she needed to.

"I'm sort of in between places, at the moment."

Not a lie, but not the whole truth, either.

"Hmm. Been there," he said. "I ain't got a phone. How come *you* ain't got a phone? All you kids got phones these days."

She reached for her cell and remembered she'd left it behind to keep Tina and Todd from tracking her. "Ah, no. I . . . I left it back home, I guess."

"Home. Hmm. Some of us never make it back."

"Back?"

Francis planted himself in a white rocking chair across from her. It was then that she noticed how his grin didn't sit quite right on his reddened face. And that he had a pistol pointed at her.

CHAPTER 10

THE SCREAM WAS not human. Quincy had never heard such a sound before, but he'd heard enough descriptions of it. And he knew exactly what that horrible cry belonged to. The lake monster. The Nietzsche Anathema.

As he approached the door to his school-skipping hideaway, Quincy wished he'd gone to class today. He'd yet to find any proof that the creature existed. Not that he didn't believe in it—he did. His heart beat in his chest to some intense tribal theme, and his mind raced with thoughts and conjured images of the Nietzsche Anathema. The book said the creature was tall like a Bigfoot. Its hands were webbed, and its eyes were as black and cold as that of a great white shark. Its mouth, armed with two little fangs, latched over its prey's lips as it suctioned away any lifeforce. It all sounded like a bizarre horror-SciFi mashup to Quincy, but that didn't make it any less possible. Not now, not at this moment when he was so alone.

He needed to go home.

He went back to the room he'd been chilling in earlier with Jester, shouldered his backpack, and hurried out the door. The sun was shining, but the warmth didn't quite reach these parts of the woods. He could stop and pull his sweatshirt from his bag, but Quincy didn't want to be out here any longer than necessary. Speeding up, he found himself in a run, suddenly sweating despite the chill. All he could hear was his feet tromping through the leaves and twigs, his breath quickening, as if all the insects and animals were sitting still and listening to him. Would they be cheering him on in silence, or hoping that the lake monster would get him? Was the creature one of them? Or was it an abomination against all of nature?

The path that lead to the road was just ahead, but something shiny lay on the ground at the head of the other path, the one he never went down, the one that led to Francis' place. The glimmer caught Quincy's attention. Walking over, he saw some kind of electronic device, too small to be a phone, and totally out of place on the forest floor. Quincy glanced around, making sure no one else was nearby. He crouched over the device and noticed a cord and headphones attached to it. It was an iPod. He'd never actually seen one before. He knew from old TV shows that they were only good for music and maybe podcasts, like the Walkmans his dad still kept in a box of old junk in the shed. He put the earbuds in and tried to figure out how to get the thing to play. He triggered the power button, and after a few seconds the screen lit up. He located the little triangle symbol that he knew was the play button. Sharp, crisp guitar chords cut through his nerves. Drums rolled in like tight little soldiers falling in line before a voice filled with snarky attitude asked if a dear mother could hear him whining.

Shock and fear gripped him as a sudden attack from behind sent him to the ground. Quincy rolled to his back, yanked the earbuds free from his ears, and propped himself up on his elbows. He stared up at Francis Owens.

"So, we finally meet," the man said.

"I was just going home," Quincy said. His gaze fell upon the gun holstered on the old man's hip.

Francis pulled the pistol free. "You should have stayed in your little shithole, Chuck. Now, your ass is mine."

"My dad will come looking for me."

"Shut up."

"My dad—"

"Boy, I know just about everything out here. You think you and your slant-eye friends can sneak up on me? Nuh-uh. Not after what you done to Tommy. Now, get the fuck up."

Quincy did as the man asked. Tears welled up behind his eyes. He tried not to show the old man how scared he was, but his body betrayed him as he stood and turned to plead with Francis. "I just want to go home. Please, I—"

"Save those tears. They don't mean shit to me. You don't think Tommy wanted to go home? When you've seen what I have—boys, your friends—drowning in their own blood, gazing out into the great nothing, ranting nonsense as they're breathing their last breaths, dying in your arms while their insides are on their outsides, you learn tears ain't gonna help save you. And they sure as hell ain't gonna keep you safe. Life ain't that way. So, you can cry all you want, and you can beg to go home, but it's not gonna do a damn thing. Get your feet moving or I'll put a bullet through your weepy snake face right here, right now."

Sobbing, a dark, wet patch spread across the front of his jeans, Quincy did as the crazy old man said. Francis laughed and shoved the barrel of the gun into Quincy's back, prodding him along. For the first time in a very long time, Quincy wondered if he'd ever see his mom again.

CHAPTER 11

MADDOX PULLED INTO the small lot of the Megill House and killed his engine. The lake, reflected in his rearview mirror, was gorgeous in the sun—but Long Lake was not the body of water belonging to his client. It held no dark secrets. At least, not the ones he was being paid to care about. Stepping from the car, he set his sunglasses on the front seat and closed the door. The Village Tavern across the road was charming. A tall, carved wooden bear stood outside its doors, welcoming all. A few little tables for outside dining stood just around the corner, so patrons could eat by the lake. No one was out there now, but Maddox decided if he were here long enough, he'd give the place a try.

Turning to the Megill House, he was in awe again. The sprawling front lawn was beautifully maintained. He inhaled the fresh cut grass, admiring the stone animal statues placed across the yard, all centered around a gorgeous fountain of a naked woman holding a dove toward the sky. The two-story building just beyond loomed like a monument all its own. Its style and size seemed out of place here, this deep in the woods. It was almost like something out of a Shirley Jackson novel. Maddox walked up the paved driveway and stepped up to the sign near the front steps.

Welcome to the Megill House. The original inn was built in 1959. Owned and operated by Chester and Henrietta Megill, the hotel served the Belgrade Lakes Region for over 30 years before a fire burned it to the ground, killing two guests and both Chester and Henrietta. Rebuilt three years later to the original's exact specifications by the late couple's daughter Virginia, and keeping with the family tradition of exceptional service, fine food, and luxurious accommodations, the Megill House has remained a top destination for travelers to Belgrade Lakes Region ever since.

He walked up the steps and through the main entrance, and was met by music coming from an unseen speaker somewhere in the room—the sound of a piano, with a beautifully rich female voice singing in accompaniment. Across the room, a young man with a trimmed beard smiled from behind a tall oak desk. The kid looked sharp in his burgundy blazer and skinny black tie.

"Hello, welcome to the Megill House. My name's Henry. How can I assist you today?"

"Ayah, Hank. Looks like I'm gonna be needing a room for the night. You got anything facing the lake?"

"Of course, sir. Let me take a look at our options."

Henry typed away, writing a novel by the sounds of it, before raising his gaze, his perfect smile still in place.

"Sir, it looks as if we do have a few options for you. We have a single suite, right at the east end of the property on the second floor that offers a brilliant view of Long Lake. It would be going at a rate of—"

"I'll take it, Hank."

"Sir?"

"It sounds great," Maddox pulled his wallet and picked the American Express card, sliding it across the desk. "Cost doesn't concern, my man. I just have to have that view."

"Of course, sir."

Hank explained the amenities and mealtimes, gave Maddox his key, and directed him to the elevator and stairs. Maddox took the key and thanked him.

Mrs. DeBaun-Owens would be picking up the bill. He might as well enjoy himself while he was here.

The room was every bit as extravagant as he'd imagined it would be. Two wide-open rooms; a four-poster, king-sized bed centered on the near wall. Across from the bed, floor-to-ceiling windows allowed the full brilliance of the daylight to infiltrate the space. Bruce closed the door and walked into the second room. An oak table stood beneath very modern looking ceiling lighting. There was a medium-sized refrigerator, the counter next to it set with glasses and bottles of champagne and wine, bourbon and tequila. A sofa faced more of the large windows, and a large television was set into the wall.

He walked to the fridge, opened it, and found a selection of beers and seltzers, waters and juices. He closed the door and picked up the bottle of bourbon. It was some fancy kind he'd never heard of. He grabbed a tumbler and poured out three fingers' worth of the whiskey. It was early in the day, but any time was a good time for a fine beverage.

He took his drink into the bedroom and gave the bathroom a quick glance before stepping to one of the windows and staring out at the glistening water. It was magnificent.

Maddox downed the bourbon in one quick swig. A fiery heat

slid down his throat to his guts, but damn if that wasn't smooth. He set the glass on the end table by the bed and headed out the door. There was work to be done. He had to find the other lake and see what Owens' money had paid for. The asshole could be out there just fishing and getting drunk, for all anyone knew. Rich people did much worse things.

Wouldn't that be something.

He smirked and nodded to Henry as he left the inn.

Rather than ask the desk clerk for directions to the Owens' property, Maddox decided to scoot into the Village Tavern and see what he could learn from the locals.

The place was dim. It wasn't a dive bar by any stretch of the imagination, but its décor brought him back down to the ground, planting his feet firmly alongside the salt-of-the-earth, regular-joe types—an arena he was much more comfortable moving around in.

He sidled up to the bar and asked the older, attractive bartender for a coffee. She gave him a quick smile, placed a brown ceramic mug on the countertop, and poured him a steaming cup.

"Thank you," he said.

"Sure thing." Her voice was somehow softer than he thought it would be. "You need anything else?"

"Nope, this'll do."

She picked up a glass and wiped it with the rag she'd slung over her slender shoulder. "Where are you coming from?"

"No place exciting."

She stopped mid-wipe. "Hmm."

He sipped his coffee and wiped his lip with the back of his hand. "What? Are you telling me you usually have world travelers zipping through here?"

"No, I mean, we get some . . . but that comes with having the Megill House right there."

"Do I look like I can afford that type of place?"

She set down the glass in her hand, tossed the rag back over her shoulder, and gave him a look over. Maddox sat up straight and stuck his chin out, giving her his most stoic smolder.

"I could see it."

"But?" he said.

"You don't talk like one of them."

"Well, you're right and wrong."

"Oh," she said.

"I'm not a world traveler, *per se*. I'm not a one-percenter. But I am booked next door. At least, for a night. But it's not exactly on my dime."

"A business trip?" She picked up the carafe and gestured to top him off.

He nodded.

She filled his mug and set the glass carafe back in place on its warmer.

"Anything interesting?"

"I'm not sure you'll find it very thrilling, but I'm here to survey one of your beautiful lakes."

"Oh, which one?"

"Owens Lake."

Maddox felt the air deflate from the room.

"What?" he asked. "Is something the matter?"

"No, no. It's just . . . "

"What?"

"Are you a ghosthunter, or one of those crypto creeps?"

"Crypto cre—oh, you mean cryptozoologist?"

"Yeah, sorry. Not creep. No offense, I mean."

"None taken. You sound like you're gonna start talking bigfoots and werewolves. Is there something I should know about that particular body of water?"

"Lake monster." A man's voice came from behind.

Maddox craned his neck and saw the man—dressed in black, jeans, a Motely Crue t-shirt, and a leather jacket despite the relative warmth—walk to the bar and take up the stool next to him. He offered a hand. Maddox noticed the two, giant star tattoos on the back of his hand. "Name's Kyle."

Maddox shook the man's hand. "You said lake monster?"

"I'll let Kyle fill you in," she said. "Belgrade has its very own creature."

"Thanks, Kelly," Kyle said.

"Okay," Maddox said. "I'll bite. What's this lake monster?"

Kyle smiled a crooked smile, ruining Maddox's eagerness.

CHAPTER 12

LEILANI 'S BRAIN WAS set on one thing—getting out of this alive. She had seen that kind of insanity in the faces of some of her foster parents. The long-gone look. Where you could tell by their eyes that not all the wires connected to all the places they should. When she was five, it had scared the shit out of her—but a decade and a bunch of nutzoid fucks later, the fear factor had lost some of its luster, taken over instead by the 'fuck this' mentality.

She pulled her lighter from her bra and sparked it. Part of her wished she had her weed right about now. She didn't need the buzz, but she sure could use the relaxation.

The dim, orange glow of the lighter ate away enough of the closet's darkness for her to get the lay of her tiny cell. She'd heard the old buzzard slide a chair across the floor and jam it in under the doorknob. Not your typical Master padlock, but effective nonetheless. She probably wasn't strong enough to muscle it open, but if she could create enough force, she may be able to knock the chair out of the way—provided he didn't have anything else keeping the chair in place. Leilani began piling the seemingly random junk on the floor to the sides. A few books and a collection of truck driver hats spilled back behind her. She quickly shoveled them out of the way. There was really no time to fuck around. Leilani had recently watched a Stephen King movie with her boyfriend, about a psychotic fan who trapped her favorite writer in her house. Leilani's mind speed-ran scene after scene of the author working out his way to freedom as she prepared to make like Paul Sheldon and skip town before she got her ankles rearranged.

She shoved her back to the shelf behind her, then exploded forward—throwing all her weight and strength into the door, shoulder-first. The lighter went out. The door rattled on impact, but brought on an ache and burn in her shoulder. It wasn't enough. She needed a different approach. She needed more weight to slam against the barricade. She sparked the lighter again, and checked the higher shelves for anything hefty. Nothing but a couple of loose bricks and some fatter hardcover books. She crouched and searched the floor but found nothing any heavier. Running on empty, she decided to poke around the darker corners, trying not to set fire to any of the old clothes he had hanging back there. A wooden baseball bat, what appeared to be more walking sticks, and—

"Holy fucking shit."

Leilani set the zippo on a clear spot on the pile beside her and reached in, wrapped her hands around the barrel of a rifle, and brought it out. She checked and found a shell chambered within.

"Are you fucking kidding me?"

She aimed the gun at the doorknob, took a deep breath, and squeezed the trigger as she exhaled. The report was deafening in the small space. She winced and dropped to a knee, the discharged rifle still clenched in her hands. The ringing stabbed her inner ears, resonating in a seemingly endless aural attack. The door, now with a fresh hole where its doorknob used to be, eased open. Freedom was just a few steps away. Wherever her captor was, surely he'd heard the gunshot. Getting to her feet, she set the gun down and did a quick search in the new light for more ammo. If it was in here, she couldn't find it. Instead, she snatched the baseball bat. It wasn't an ideal weapon against a pistol, but beggars can't be assholes. You make the best with the shitty hand you're dealt. Leilani had a whole life of scars and practice on that score.

She stepped from the closet just in time to see the door open. For inexplicable reasons, she quickly set the baseball bat behind the back of the couch. Her brow knit as a boy with orangish curly hair, dressed in a checked pastel pink and green checked shirt and blue jeans, entered the house. His face was red. His eyes found her gaze, and she could tell he'd been crying. He hung his head. The pistol-packing old man followed, his weapon aimed at her.

"Did you miss me?"

Leilani didn't answer. She watched his movements, looking for any weakness to target.

"My dad's going to come looking for me," the boy said, his hands shaking at his sides.

"Yeah, bring on your whole cock-sucking platoon. The more the fucking merrier. Now, shut up and get over there with the whore."

The boy stood, his eyes glassing over.

The old man stepped to the kid's face. "Yeah, go on. Give me more of them tears. Shit, you think I'm scary. Do I frighten you?"

The boy was nodding. Leilani watched a tear roll down his cheek. She wanted to clobber this old fuck, right now.

Quick as a lightning strike, the man brought the weapon up and pistol whipped the boy on the top of his head, dropping the kid to the floor.

"Come on," he yelled. "Get up. On your feet, soldier. You can't take that, you're in for some real trouble out here. The rest of my men won't be so nice."

Leilani stepped behind the couch, quickly glancing at the bat leaning there. She turned her attention back to the man hovering over the boy. Blood flowed from the fresh wound on the kid's forehead.

"Leave him alone!"

The old man craned his neck. "Oh, don't you go getting all jealous. Old Francis has got plenty in store for you, too." He spat on the boy and started her way.

"Why are you doing this?" she said. Her left hand moved toward the bat.

"You stepped into the wrong jungle, honey . . . "

He seemed to drift off somewhere in his mind. She eyed the pistol in his hand, the weapon looking like a snake coiled to strike.

"Just let us go and we'll never come out here again," she said.

His consciousness seemed to pour back into his gaze as he found hers. "Too late for that, I'm afraid." Francis raised the gun. And fired.

Leilani closed her eyes, waiting for the bullet. But it never came.

The gunshot was deafening in the small cabin. Leilani gasped but felt no pain.

She opened her eyes in time to see the old man hit the floor, the gun sliding from his hand. The boy stood above him..

"Come on!" the kid said, reaching out a hand for her.

She grabbed the bat and stepped back from behind the couch.

"What are you doing?" the boy asked.

"You two are gonna pay for this," Francis growled from where he lay sprawled upon the floor. He was reaching for the pistol, his hand trembling

Leilani brought the bat down on his back.

"Garrrghhh!"

She hit him again and again, the last blow finding the back of his head. His body stilled. She turned to the boy. "Do you know how to get us out of here?"

The boy stared at the man on the floor.

"Hey, kid."

"What? I . . . do you think you killed him?"

"No. I don't think so." She handed the boy the bat.

He took it. "What are you doing?"

She stepped over Francis' back and bent over. Her hand found the pistol's handle. She stood and stepped to the boy. "Now we have the upper hand if he somehow catches up to us. Let's go."

As they stepped outside, Leilani closed the door behind them. "What's your name?"

"Quincy."

"Hi, Quincy. I'm Leilani. Now, which way do we go?"

They had started on a path leading deeper into the woods when they heard Francis crashing through the trees behind them.

"He's gonna get you! You hear me? If I don't catch you first, he's gonna make you wish I did!"

"What's he talking about?"

Quincy shouldered the bat and picked up speed. "I . . . I don't know. Let's just hurry."

"He's yelling about someone else getting us. Who else is out here?"

The screech from up ahead froze them both in place.

CHAPTER 13

THE SKEEZY-LOOKING MAN across from Maddox downed his morning Budweiser, washing back a fistful of peanuts before beginning his story.

"They say the creature was here before Owens bought the pond and all the acreage surrounding it. Lot of locals would have you believe the bad shit started when that scumbag rich boy and his greedy wife scooped the land up before the town could buy it and preserve it for future generations, but that's only part of what happened."

"What's out there?" Maddox asked, the coffee in his hand forgotten.

Kyle pulled a cigarette from the pack upon the table. He twirled it between his thumb and forefinger. "It lives beneath the lake."

"What does?"

The man's squinty gaze rose from the cigarette in his hand, to Maddox. "It has a name. One given to it more than thirty years ago. Someone called it the 'Nietzsche Anathema'. It was here before that, but it wasn't until the Owens group came along and upset the balance of nature that it really started . . . killing."

Maddox wasn't sure if Kyle was a complete kook or if it was possible that this small Maine village really held a dark secret out in the woods. He'd heard and seen plenty of fucking weird shit, but monsters? No. Not ones that didn't hide within the confines of human flesh, that is.

"Are there pictures? Videos?"

"Ah," Kyle said, sticking the unlit cigarette between his slim lips. "A non-believer, I take it."

"How's that?"

"You're one of them atheists, aren't ya?"

"Not that it matters here, but yeah, me and God are a little at odds when it comes to free will, the creation of the universe, and heaven and hell, I suppose."

"Sometimes, Mr. Maddox, you gotta put your faith in something. You've gotta trust in what you cannot see. You best trust that this monster is fucking real. You forget that, you scoff at that, and you go traipsin' out in them woods 'round that pond, you're gonna say 'Kyle was right', and that's probably the last thought you'll have before it takes your soul."

Maddox would not believe in bullshit creatures from the lake. What he would believe is that Henry Owens owned more than the land around here.

"You know if Mr. Owens has a cabin out there?"

Kyle nodded.

"You think you can tell me how to find it?"

"I could, but it won't do no good."

"Why? Because of your lake monster?"

"If the Neitzsche Anathema don't get you, Francis'll probably blow your head off."

"Francis?"

"Henry Owens' brother. That crazy Vietnam vet is the only one lives out there. Nobody else is dumb enough."

"I take it Francis isn't what you'd call friendly?"

"He'll shoot you where you stand. He don't trust no one. No one 'cept his brother."

"So, Owens probably takes care of Francis' home, food, supplies, all that jazz, and in return Francis acts as a sort of deterrent for anyone thinking about coming out to the property."

"You'd probably be right on all that, 'cept it ain't just Francis that keeps the rats from the cheese out there."

"Oh yeah, your lake monster."

"I can see you ain't gonna listen to me. Not many do about much, but you'd be best served to this one time, Mr. Smarty-Pants." Kyle slid his chair back from the table so suddenly that Maddox jumped. "You go on ahead and see for yourself. You fucking city folk know every goddamn thing." Kyle pulled a lighter from his shirt pocket and lit the cigarette before he'd made it to the door.

"Kyle," Tabitha said. "I told you, you can't light those in here."

Maddox stood and walked back to the bar. "How about you?"

She looked at him. "How about me what?"

"You believe in this creature, too?"

She took a step back, folded her arms across her chest. Her gaze dipped to her feet. Her fingers found an oblong black stone hanging from a thin chain around her neck.

"My uncle gave me this so long ago it seems more like something I saw in a movie than it does real life, ya know?"

"What is it?"

"Onyx, I think."

Maddox took another sip of his coffee. "Does it mean anything?"

She twirled the stone between her fingers for a second and let it go. "Nah, maybe. I don't really know." Her eyes, prettier than he first thought, the way they appeared to smile on their own, met his. "I just remember thinking it was really cool. He took it off then and there and put it around my neck."

"Let me guess, your uncle's the monster hunter in the family?"

"Him and his friend went out there to fish. Never heard that there was fish in a manmade pond, especially that one, but they were young and dumb and drunk, so they went to see for themselves. My uncle never made it back. His friend Clark did, though. Told us all what happened. Said Uncle Steve had refused to go out on the canoe once they were out there. Clark left him on the shore and went out anyway. Said he was out there maybe fifteen minutes when he noticed Uncle Steve start acting strange on the shore. Said he saw him staring into the woods like someone was coming. He didn't run. Didn't try and signal Clark—he just started freaking out and pacing back and forth. Clark started making his way to shore when it came from the lake and attacked my uncle."

"What came from the lake? This . . . creature?"

"You can choose to believe or not to believe, but that won't matter if you go out there. Monsters don't need you to believe in them. You're just safer if you do."

"If I wanted to have Clark corroborate this story, where could I find him?"

"Megill Cemetery."

"He the caretaker or something?"

"Clark killed himself right after Uncle Steve's funeral."

Maddox left The Village Tavern and headed across the street. The light of day felt good as he made his way to his car. He didn't believe in ghost stories or monsters under the bed, in the closet or in the lake, but these folks had given him goosebumps. They certainly seemed to believe their nonsense. Small-town minds tended to be less scientific or reasonable, and therefore were more prone to putting faith in folktales. It was truly amazing the human species ever made it out of the Dark Ages.

His cellphone rang as he started his car.

"Hello, Mrs. Owens."

"I trust you have something to report. You'd better, after that stunt you pulled."

"Yeah, sorry about that."

"I'm sure you're not. So, what do you have for me?"

"I'm checking on a few things. I should have a better idea by tonight."

"And you're staying at the Megill House, I see."

Maddox checked his rearview and scanned the lot. He'd known she would find out he was here, but he'd figured it would only be when he gave her the bill. "Indeed," he said. "Shouldn't be for more than a night or two."

"You think my husband stayed there? Tell me, Mr. Maddox. Do you think Henry's still alive?"

He hadn't really gotten that far. "I do," he lied.

"I'll expect a full report tonight over a glass of wine."

This woman was used to getting what she wanted. Normally, he'd consider fucking his employer. He'd done it plenty of times before, and Mrs. DeBaun-Owens was attractive. There was just something about her that he could not fucking stand. He didn't trust her, sure—but he rarely trusted anyone. It was something darker he couldn't quite put his finger on.

"Sounds perfect," he said.

"Good. Let's say eight o'clock. Your room."

"I'll be waiting."

"Goodbye, Mr. Maddox."

CHAPTER 14

QUINCY GRABBED LEILANI by the shoulder and shoved her toward an overgrown path, away from the lake. Better to head for the straightest way out over the easiest. Quincy was betting Francis wasn't in good enough shape to battle the thicker parts of his neighborhood.

They were barely a hundred feet in when Leilani dropped from sight and began screaming.

Quincy stepped to the end of the shallow pit and nearly screeched himself. Rats, dozens of them, crawled and squealed around the bottom of the ten or so wooden spikes sticking up from the ground. Leilani had one of the horrifying spears sticking up through her foot. She was lucky not to have been completely impaled. Blood was also dripping heavily from a gouge in her right forearm.

"My fucking foot, *ow*, goddamn, my fucking foot. Get me out of here!" she cried.

The rats were already beginning to surround her.

"Do you have the gun?" he asked.

"What?"

"The gun that you took from Francis."

"It's down here. Gah! Fuck, fuck, fuck! Just help get me out. Quick!"

Quincy's stomach tumbled. When his mother gashed her hand open on a broken glass two years back, he'd passed out at the sight of so much blood. He was getting lightheaded now watching Leilani bloody forearm.

"Hey! Kid, don't pass out on me."

After a few seconds, Quincy shook free from the sick feeling, and came back to the moment. "Give me your hand," he said.

She reached up and grabbed hold of him.

Her cries stopped them both. She let go.

"You're going to have to get your foot free."

She covered her eyes with the inside of her elbow. "Oh my God, this fucking hurts."

"I need to help you, then. If you were free, I might be able to pull you out, but if you can't do it yourself, we're going to need a ladder. I bet Francis has one."

"Wait, what? You're not leaving me here."

"If I jump down there, we'll both be stuck. I'll run."

"No!"

"I'll be quick."

"What if he finds me?"

He scanned the pit. "There," he said, pointing a few feet ahead of her. "Can you reach the gun?"

Leilani bent forward, reaching out, her fingertips inches from the weapon.

"Can you get it?"

She tried again, groaning as she stretched. Quincy winced watching her move in obvious pain. After a second try, Leilani snagged the barrel and pulled the gun to her chest, panting and visibly sweating from the effort. "Got it. Please hurry."

"I will."

Quincy bolted from the path. No sooner had he left the beaten trail than a sharp cry exploded from somewhere off to his right. Anxiety spilled through his intestines like cold oil.

The pain was like a thousand fires flaring up at once, constantly searing the flesh and inner workings of her foot. The pain in her forearm and shin was bad, too, but paled in comparison. All three torn and tattered parts of her body were bleeding profusely. Leilani waited for the rodents scurrying over her feet to turn vampiric and feed on her wounds. The rats kept back for the time being—a small relief for her. She sucked air through her teeth, sweating through her t-shirt as she gripped the pistol. She felt like a sitting duck, and didn't like it.

The god-awful, human-like screech decided her next move for her.

"Ewargghhh!" she cried as she tried to lean forward. She bit her lips and sunk her fingernails into the palms of her hands. The fresh batch of pain from her injured forearm caused her to go weak in the knees again. Her foot burned from the inside out and scorched every inch of flesh around the dirty spike poking up through her sneaker. Taking deep breaths, telling herself it was *abso-fucking-lutely* necessary, she put the gun in the front of her jeans, cupped her hands beneath her sweaty knee. She gritted her teeth, summoned what strength she had left, and yanked. Suns exploded within the cosmos of her rent flesh. Tears streaked her face.

"Hi, honey. I'm home." Francis looked down on her from the edge of the pit. "Did ya miss me?"

She bent further at the waist in an attempt to conceal the gun. Had he not seen it? Her back to the old man, Leilani pulled her t-shirt over the pistol.

"Nice of you to check and make sure I was still alive," he said. "You know, that's the least you can do after clobbering someone over the head with a bat."

"Fuck you!"

He spat down at her. A nasty glob of mucus splattered her nose, and bits of spittle landed on her teeth.

"Get me out of here!" she screamed.

"Shh, shh," he said. His gaze traced the outline of the top of the pit. "This here is what your VC brothers would use to surprise us. Nice, huh? Yeah, we'd have one of 'em sniping us from the trees ahead there. While we tried to creep closer to kill the sneaky bastard, one or two of us grunts would find one of these plunger pits the hard way. Like you."

She wanted to pull the gun and shut the motherfucker up.

"*Punji* sticks," he continued. "You bastards used to dig these pits, some as shallow as three feet, others a little deeper like this one, and cover the floor of them with sharpened bamboo. We'd fall in and be fucked. You smell that shit down there with you? It ain't from the rats. I smeared the tips of some of those spikes with my own feces. I pissed on the rest. If you're lucky enough not to catch one of them spikes through your gut or head or throat, you get to battle off a nasty fucking infection. You're welcome."

"Why are you doing this?"

"This is my world out here. You miss the signs?"

Leilani couldn't put weight on her savaged foot. She leaned against the dirt wall, the rats still tumbling around her ankles. The feeling of their fur and feet scampering across her skin made her queasy.

"What's the matter? Can't you read?"

The skin-crawling wail came again. This time it sounded much closer. The smug look on the old man's face crumbled into something less assured. He began blinking and shaking his head, like someone just waking up in the morning.

What the fuck is with this guy?

Francis wiped his mouth with a shaky hand before looking to her. His brow scrunched down in confusion. "What's . . . ?" he sounded lost.

"Get me out of here," she repeated.

Francis turning his gaze back to her, still blinking. When he spoke again, his voice was different, urgent. He got down on a knee and reached a hand out to her. "Do you want to take your chances with that thing, or do you want to live to see another day?"

Leilani's lip quivered.

"Come on. I'm offering you a chance. *He* ain't gonna do that."

Leilani took the old man's hand.

A branch cracked somewhere by the lake. They both sucked in a breath and whipped their heads in that direction.

CHAPTER 15

MADDOX STOPPED HIS car at the slightly overgrown entryway. Signs littered the surrounding trees. ***No Trespassing*** and ***Private Property***.

The gate was nothing more than a rusty chain attached to two concrete posts. Maddox got out and pulled a set of bolt cutters from his trunk, then walked up to the padlock and snipped it free. The Master lock thudded to the dirt below as the chain rattled and followed it down. He took the lock and tossed it to the side, then dragged the chain out of the way and piled it next to one of the posts.

Back in his vehicle, Maddox drove on, watching the dirt road and surrounding forest go by his window. The grass was as high as the hood of the car in most places, making the slim road hard to follow. Moss in various shades of green and pale blue lichen covered trees like fungal alien species here to conquer and multiply. Maddox couldn't recall the last time he'd been out in nature like this, where it felt like if he went in too far the road would get swallowed up behind him and he'd never find his way out. It was disorienting. A bright glistening hit his sight as the water became visible in the distance, shining through a sea of outstretched branches. Finally, a well-beaten road appeared. He pulled onto it and followed it left, around the lake. More of the same signage warned him that he shouldn't be here.

"Yeah, I know. Beware the lake monster."

The road climbed higher and led him to a clearing cut into the right side of the road. Maddox parked and got out of the car. There was a white Chevy truck sitting there. He walked to the window and glanced inside. A hardhat, some manila folders with smudged fingerprints, and a thermos covered the bench seat. There was a tan purse on the floor, and . . . a tire iron. Maddox opened the door, and saw the dark red stain beneath the tire iron. Stepping back, he closed the truck door and gazed around the immediate area.

He stepped to the front of the vehicle and found a walking path. He followed it to a larger clearing that led to a precipice overlooking the lake. The drop was maybe thirty feet or so. He could picture local kids run-jumping down from here in the summers. He'd had a spot just like this when he was a kid. He and his friends called it 'the Falls'. For all the dumb stunts they'd pulled there, the only incident that he remembered was when a girl named Jessica disappeared. Everybody suspected her boyfriend, but no remains were ever found, and no charges were ever laid.

So, the Chevy was out here alone, abandoned, a bloody weapon inside. At a perfect murder spot, here by a lake that no one dared to visit. Was it possible whoever owned that truck had something to do with Henry Owens' disappearance?

Maddox returned to the Chevy. He opened the folder and found a bunch of papers with the heading for a place called O'Connor's Motors. It meant nothing to him. He tossed the greasy papers and folder aside and went for the purse.

"Holy shit."

He held an office badge belonging to one Deana Marston for the Henry Owens building in Augusta.

A connection.

His gaze dropped to the tire iron and the small stain beneath it. The registration in the glove box said the truck belonged to a Kevin Marston. Most likely Deana's husband. Next, Maddox moved to the truck bed and found a small burlap bag containing zip ties and duct tape. He was back up front looking beneath the driver's seat when a strange cry echoed through the woods. He stood as gooseflesh came to life across the backs of his arms. That sound wasn't human. It was something else. He'd be hard-pressed to guess what kind of animal screeched that way.

Kyle's lake monster came to mind.

No such thing.

The awful cry could have come from anywhere. The echo crossed the lake from parts unknown. As Maddox stepped away from the truck, a glint of sunlight reflected from the ground beneath him. He crouched and found a set of keys. A giant ***K*** dangled from the ring along with six keys, one of which he knew belonged to the Chevy. The vehicle wasn't abandoned—and Maddox was positive the driver wasn't somewhere out here wandering around. This was a crime scene. And now regardless of his innocence, should the police look it over, his fingerprints would be all over the place.

Maddox walked to his car and grabbed two five-gallon gas cans from his trunk. He carried them to the Chevy and placed them in the truck bed. He'd found all the information he needed. He wanted to drive around the rest of the lake area and see if he could find any of the missing.

Following the path around the lake, it didn't take long before he heard a girl crying out for help.

CHAPTER 16

QUINCY NEVER MADE it to the cabin.

Hearing the creature's cry, he rushed to the main trail. Less than a hundred feet away, the lake monster stepped from the trees and stopped in the center of the path. Its sudden appearance turned every bone in his body to jelly. Dropping to the ground, he began to shake as he watched the abomination reveal itself. Francis appeared opposite the creature, stepping to the thing like a trainer at a circus might approach its animal—cautiously fearful. The monster towered over the old man. Its skin was dark and scaly, and its face was a nightmare come to life. Its circular mouth puckered. Four sharp, hook-like teeth did the talking for the beast.

"Get back!" Francis said, standing up straight and holding his palms out toward the creature.

It hesitated for only few seconds before lumbering at the old man, trying to latch its webbed hands around him. Francis picked up the baseball bat and swung at the beast, catching it in the shoulder and knocking it back.

Quincy sucked in a breath. He felt like he was being returned to his body from a darkened theater of a Saturday matinee creature feature. The Nietzsche Anathema was out of his library book and standing here now in real life.

Francis swung again but whiffed. The monster latched onto one of his arms and began to tussle with him. Francis jerked like a fish caught in a net. Quincy gasped as the creature pulled Francis's arm until the limb came free from the rest of the old man's body. Horrified, Quincy's complexion paled at the monster's strength. It took another few seconds for him to notice the lack of blood from the severed limb.

It's a prosthetic.

The creature held the appendage in its grasp turning its head to the side.

Francis used the moment to charge the monster, dropping a shoulder and knocking it to the ground.

"Hurry!" he yelled, standing and facing Quincy. He gestured to the hole. "Don't just stand there. *Get her the hell out of there!*"

Quincy wasn't sure what to make of the old man's sudden change of personality. Why was he helping them?

The creature wasn't done with them yet. It rose and dropped the prosthetic arm to the ground before arching its back and letting loose another wail.

"Get her out, *now*!"

Quincy ran to the pit. Leilani was drenched in sweat and looked ready to pass out. Quincy offered his hand.

She grimaced and took it.

The girl was heavier than he'd thought she would be, but with no choice, Quincy pulled as hard as he could. With Leilani using her good arm and good leg to help, he yanked her from the pit.

In the jungle, the monsters were hiding everywhere—in the trees, underfoot, beneath the surface of lily pad death swamps. The thing in his brother's lake was good at being invisible when it wanted to be—but sometimes it got rambunctious and came for anything out here that moved. Just like the VC, it could be cold, calculating, and was willing to tear trespassers to shreds.

Francis had never been this close to the creature. Gazing into its beady onyx eyes, his heart jackhammered in his chest until his remaining limbs began to tingle. The thing's breath reeked of stagnant water and rotten vegetation. Its strange mouth contained horrid little teeth, all curved to needle-like points. They were now mere inches from his face. Francis knew fear, he knew bravery, he knew stupidity. All three were colliding, smashing a black hole into the quiet world where he'd secluded himself over the last three decades. It was all coming to this. In this moment, everything in his head was mixed up. A momentary lack of reason and sense. He'd slipped mentally over the years with some episodes lasting only minutes while others stretched out longer and longer.

The monster was strong, but even with only one good arm Francis still had enough fight in him to make it tough for the thing to best him. It screeched again, and its wet, slimy saliva hit Francis' cheeks, lips, and throat. Wrapped in the creature's scaly arms, his breaths fired in short bursts as it squeezed. Ribs snapped, pain exploding inside. He managed a glance in the direction of the pit, and saw the two teens watching, drop-jawed and paralyzed by what they were witnessing. He thought of Tommy Murphy. A kid with a young wife and a baby on the way. A kid with a life full of dreams ahead of him. Tommy: sprawled out in the mud and rain, his insides spilling to the ground, the bottom half of his body four feet from the rest of him. Tommy's mouth filled with blood and words that no longer made sense.

Francis tried to tell the kids to run, but it only came out in a croaked groan.

With his last gasp of strength, Francis leaned his head back and then brought his forehead crashing into the creature's ugly face, as hard as he could.

The lake monster let out a small cry, its grip easing slightly, before rage spilled from its maw and Francis felt himself cast away. First he was sailing backwards, and then his body found the *punji* sticks.

Francis' moans spilled curdled milk into Quincy's stomach. The Nietzsche Anathema stood at the opposite edge of the pit, huffing and puffing like the big bad wolf. Francis gave one last gasp and lay still. Splotches of crimson blossomed through his clothing. It seemed impossible now that the one-armed, elderly man in that hole could have harmed them earlier.

"Come on," Leilani said. "Let's go."

CHAPTER 17

MADDOX SAW THE creature and tried unsuccessfully to convince his brain that it was just a man in a costume.

"Get up," a boy said.

A young woman struggled to her feet as the monster ran at them.

Maddox was in a full sprint, the gun strapped to the outside of his calf forgotten.

Two shots rang out.

The creature fell to a knee as Maddox came crashing into it, knocking it all the way down to the ground. Its skin was slimy and cold; it smelled like something that had died in the water and been left to rot. He struggled against the creature as it let out one of those god-awful shrieks he'd heard echoing around the lake. Rolling to a stop, the thing placed its webbed hands on either side of his face. He slammed his fists into the thing's sides, to little effect.

"Leilani, don't," a boy said behind him.

"Get out of here," Maddox said as he struggled to keep the monster occupied.

"Let me kill it," the girl said.

Maddox remembered the gun at his ankle, but the creature's face came straight at his before he could reach for the weapon. Four sharp hooks punctured his face just above and beneath his lips, and a tight suctioning encased his mouth. He managed one breath through his nose before a rush of foul water burst from the creature's enclosed maw and flooded his throat. Gagging and drowning on dry land, water running from his nose, Maddox convulsed in the creature's grasp.

He was going under, disappearing in his mind. When the gunshots came again, it was as if he were already in the depths of the cold, dark lake, in the arms of the thing that could not be.

CHAPTER 18

LEILANI EMPTIED THE WEAPON, no longer caring if any of the bullets struck the man who'd come out of nowhere to attack the creature. She didn't stop pulling the clicking trigger until Quincy twisted the spent weapon from her trembling hands.

"We need to go. *Now!*" he said.

He didn't wait for her response. She felt him pushing and pulling her away, holding her up as she tumbled left, her foot flaring as she cried out in pain. Glancing back, one arm hooked around his neck, Leilani saw the monster roll off the mystery man and struggle to get to its feet. She'd hurt it. Hopefully, it would die. She didn't want to be around to find out. She wanted to go home. To Todd and Tina. If they'd have her back.

She gripped Quincy, inhaling the smell of his sweat, appreciating his presence. Where would she be right now? What would have happened had he not been out here today, as well? Francis was dead. Whatever had been wrong with the man—his delusions, his confusion—he didn't deserve the death he received. Whatever the case, Leilani didn't want to be next.

The trail rounded a corner to a wider path.

"Is this the way out?" she asked.

"Not exactly."

"Not exactly? What the hell is that supposed to mean? Where are we going?"

"There's another cabin out here."

She wanted to stop and yell at him for being so goddamn naive, but she didn't want to help the thing catch up to them, either.

"My backpack is there. My phone. We can call for help."

Her injuries slowed them, but so did the fact that this area of the woods was so dense out here. Eventually, the cabin came into sight. It was slightly smaller than Francis' place, yet somehow appeared less abandoned. Quincy got her to the steps, and she took hold of the small handrail. She'd either gotten used to the pain in her foot—the damn thing was losing feeling—or something worse was happening internally. She felt blessed for the slight reprieve, but chose to hold back the fear that she could lose the foot. If what Francis had told her was true, and he had indeed covered the *punji* stick with his own shit and piss (and she didn't see the point in his lying about such a thing), the wound was definitely going to be infected.

"Stay right here—"

"No," she said, clutching his forearm. "Don't leave me out here."

"Okay."

She met his gaze, and noticed more kindness in his brown eyes than she'd seen in someone else her age.

He helped her to the door and through the entryway.

"I'll stand guard," she said. "Go find your phone."

Staring out the open door, toward the trail, she noticed the shadows growing long to the west. It would be dark soon. And she sure as fuck didn't want to be out here with that thing in the night.

"Quincy, hurry up."

He walked to the spot where Jester usually hustled for crumbs, and remembered something terrible—he'd taken his bag when he'd gone out. He'd dropped it on the trail when the old man stopped him.

Quincy walked to the doorway and stared at the beautiful girl gazing out the front door. Her black hair mostly pulled back; a few loose strands framing her beautiful mocha skin. Even sweaty, dirty, and beat up, she looked great. There was blood dried and caked to her arm, down one of her shins and covering her punctured sneaker. She'd been through hell, and now he had to tell her they were on their own. There was no rescue coming. They were going to have to try and make it out of the woods alone.

She turned and looked at him. He watched her gaze drop to his empty hands and watched the slight upturn at the corners of her mouth fall with the acknowledgement.

He shook his head and dropped his chin.

"I forgot . . . I had it with me . . . then Francis . . . ."

"It's all right," she said. "A lot of crazy shit just happened. It's not the end of the world. But we better decide what we're doing. Its already getting dark out."

"Do you think it's still alive?"

She hopped out the front door and took a seat on the porch steps. The shadows around her were expanding with every passing moment. "I don't even know what the hell *it* is."

CHAPTER 19

GASPING FOR AIR, coughing up whatever vile fluid the creature tried to kill him with, Maddox crawled for the trees. It was gone. He wasn't sure where to, but right now he couldn't give a fuck. All he knew was that he was still alive, and lucky to be so. The shadows wouldn't hide him long, but he needed a moment to collect himself. Glancing over his shoulder and around the base of the pine tree, there was no sign of the creature or of the teens. Had it chased after them? Had it returned to the lake? Was it dead?

Every breath brought fiery pain. Wounded but still breathing, Maddox knew it wasn't good. He could only manage shallow breaths. His lungs were fucked. Whether the damage was permanent, he couldn't say. He could feel four sore spots around his mouth where the thing had punctured him with its hideous teeth. Maddox used the bottom of his shirt to wipe the blood from his face. He found more crimson stains in two spots along his shirt and pants. He lifted his shirt and found his flesh beneath unblemished. The blood was not his. Maddox pulled up his pantleg and grabbed the pistol. If that goddam thing was still out here, he was going to kill the shit out of it. And if he was lucky enough to make it out of this, he owed Kyle and Kelly back at that bar a couple drinks. First things first. He stood and turned off the safety on his Glock. Stepping from the tree, Maddox walked to the edge of the shallow pit where he'd seen the teens. A man lay dead, impaled on a bunch of spikes. It was a Vietnam-style trap. He'd seen them in countless movies. He couldn't think of what they were called, but like all the traps of that war, or 'conflict' if you wanted to go by how the US preferred to remember it, this was nasty. The hole was maybe five feet deep, filled with sharpened branches and crawling with rats. Maddox couldn't verify it, but he'd be willing to bet the dead old man was Francis Owens, and this was probably his own trap.

"Thank you for your service, sir."

Maddox held the butt of the gun close to his chest, barrel pointed out as he hurried toward the path, his eyes scanning the ground for other possible booby traps. He didn't want any spikes slamming through his body.

A little way up the path, he had to take a knee. His chest was on fire, and it was getting harder and harder to breathe. His stomach turned on him. He retched and splattered the soil with his breakfast. Eyes wide open, Maddox fell back on his ass. There was a horrid mixture of blood, stomach acid, and something that looked an awful lot like used motor oil in his vomit. The sight brought another bout of retching. He wiped his mouth with his forearm, his hand trembling, and climbed to his feet. His bones heavy, his muscles sore, Maddox raised his chin to the sky. It was almost dark.

CHAPTER 20

"I THINK WE can make it to my house."

Leilani looked at the bloody mess that was her foot. "I don't think I can."

"It's maybe fifteen minutes from here. I can help you."

"Could take twice as long with me and this," she nodded at her foot.

"We can do it."

"I think you should go without me."

"What?" Quincy looked like someone had just asked to euthanize his pet. "No. Are you crazy? You can't stay here. It's going to come for you."

"Believe me, I don't want to stay any more than you want me to, but the sooner you go, the better. You'll be faster. Get home and call the police."

"What if—"

"Go."

"Are you sure?"

"Yes," she reached out and squeezed his shoulder. "Go. Just hurry, please."

He nodded. "Okay. Okay. You should block this door after I'm out."

Leilani watched until the shadows gulped him up into nothingness. They'd used an old loveseat and two bureaus to barricade the front entrance. She'd jammed an uncomfortable-looking plastic school chair beneath the knob on the more modern-looking backdoor. She was grateful for Quincy helping her with the stuff for the front barricade, but now that she was all alone, she couldn't help but think of the time it took away from his getting home.

Silence surrounded her like a diseased blanket. Millipedes trampled through her intestines, sweat spawned in droplets along her spine. Leilani tried to just breath. There was no reason to go catastrophic yet. She'd filled that fucking creature with lead. This wasn't a horror movie. There was no coming back from the dead.

But did I kill it?

Somewhere in her head, she could imagine a keyboard playing the theme from John Carpenter's *Halloween*.

"Stop it," she said aloud. "Stop freaking yourself out. There's nothing out there."

A rattle, almost like a child's toy with plastic wheels being dragged across a hardwood floor, came to life behind her. She spun and let out a quick squeak. In the dying light, she sighed as a squirrel emerged, dragging something with him that she couldn't quite make out.

She made to stand when a pain, like a tooth through the lip, came to life in her ravaged foot. A hurt so immense she fell and crawled backwards to the wall, holding her foot out as far from the rest of her body as she could, as if she could mitigate the pain by keeping the source at a safe distance. She moaned in agony, feeling nauseous and on the verge of passing the fuck out.

The sudden banging on the front door seized her heart.

Leilani's entire body shivered and shook as she tried to contain everything at once. The tremors brought tears to her eyes. Holding her breath, she winced and gritted her teeth against the still-bursting hurt in her foot. If it didn't subside soon, she was not going to be able to hold back the scream building inside of her. The pounding on the door grew louder. She could feel the earthquaking tremors through the floor.

Beads of sweat rolled down her forehead, one hung from the end of her nose and dripped to her top lip. The hurt was going to devour her.

The banging on the front stopped. The quiet raised every hair on her body in alert. How long had it been since Quincy left? Her gaze fell upon an open window in the room next to her. She swallowed hard, and began dragging herself in that direction.

A screech stopped her in her tracks.

CHAPTER 21

QUINCY STUMBLED ONTO his lawn just as headlights spilled across the yard and a vehicle pulled into the driveway.

"Dad!"

The driver's door opened, and his father hopped out the truck with the engine still running.

"What in the hell are you doing?" his dad asked, hurrying to Quincy's side.

Quincy could smell the booze on his father's breath, but the man's intoxication was the least of his concerns. He was winded, but he blurted out, "We have to call the cops. There's a girl in trouble out near the lake. At one of the cabins."

"Were you at school today?"

"What?"

"You heard me. You skip school again?"

"Dad, yes, but it's not important right now—"

"Boy, I do not know what makes you think you can do whatever the hell you want around here but if you don't—"

Quincy stood and stepped to his father's face. He was only thirteen, but already stood eye to eye with the man. "It. Doesn't. *Matter*. There's a girl in trouble. If we don't get her help she's going to die."

That seemed to get through to the man—barely.

Quincy held out his hand. "Give me your phone."

In the darkness of the woods, Maddox found his way along the path and came to a cabin. The creature's wail erupted from up ahead. It was way too fucking close. Staring ahead in the night, trying to spot the horrid thing before it could find him, each breath burned like it was his last cigarette—too hot and too fast.

He double-checked that the safety was off on his Glock, and pushed forward. Moonlight outlined the path to the cabin. The hairs on the back of his neck stood, antenna seeking out electric waves from a monster that had no right to exist. Maddox could still taste the foul, bottom-feeding sediment and filth the disgusting beast had tried to drown him in, and still feel the ghosts of its strong, scaly arms around him. The violation would be avenged. He might die in the process, but he wasn't taking that final coffin nail without taking this thing with him. The hows, whats, and whys surrounding the whereabouts of Henry Owens were no longer his fucking concern.

Maddox found the front door to the cabin and stopped. Sweat seemed to be oozing from every one of his pores. His intestines were threatening betrayal again, and his head felt as though someone were violently attempting to crack the front of his skull open with Thor's hammer, Mjolnir. There was no doubting the finality of his current situation. The body never lies. This was his own end game.

Leilani peered out the window, her eyes just cresting the sill. It wasn't a matter of *if* the creature could get in but *when*. She just didn't want to be totally blind-sided. Not that that should matter. Her injuries weren't going to allow her to put up much of a fight. If Quincy wasn't on his way back with help, she was dead fucking meat.

"Come on out, you fucking chicken-shit beast."

Holy shit.

Gripping the lip of the windowsill, perspiring and shaky, suddenly hopeful, she struggled to her good foot. Squinting to see in the darkness beyond, she could make out a shape at the edge of the driveway. Somebody was out there.

The creature rose directly on the other side of the glass and cried out. Flashes of light and gunshots exploded from the shadows. The window above her head shattered, raining shards upon her as she fell backwards, and chaos unleashed around her.

CHAPTER 22

"GET BACK HERE with my phone! Quincy!"

He should've known his father wouldn't believe him. He never gave a crap about anything that wasn't his beer or his girlfriend. It might not be a hundred percent fair or accurate, but that didn't matter. Leilani didn't have time for Quincy to explain it all to his dad.

His sneakers slapped the blacktop as left his backyard for Burch Lane Road on his way toward the lake. He could hear his dad shouting: *"Stop, or get your ass kicked!"*

Quincy had always been afraid of the dark. He'd always been afraid of his dad, too—but tonight, none of it mattered. He'd left a wounded girl behind. He'd never be able to live with himself if anything else happened to her.

He dared a look back before heading off the road and into the woods again. His father was still giving chase and closing the gap.

Quincy took the moment to dial 9-1-1 and then bolted down the path he used to get to the cabin.

"9-1-1, what's your emergency?"

"There've been gunshots at the cabins around Owens Lake. Hurry, Francis Owens is dead."

"Son, I need you to remain calm. Are you in immediate danger? Can you get someplace safe?"

"Just send help. Hurry."

"Help is—"

Quincy ended the call and stuffed his dad's phone in his pocket. It would only take him a few minutes to get back to Leilani.

His father's calls to him were fading. Either he'd lost him on the path, or the man's dad-bod was slowing him down. Whatever the case, Quincy forced himself to move faster. *How quickly would the Augusta PD or the State Troopers arrive?* Would they even believe him? What if no one showed up?

A few minutes later, the unmistakable sound of gunshots rang out, causing Quincy to drop to his knees.

Glass shattered and Leilani screamed.

Quincy raced toward the sounds of violence.

The silhouette of the cabin came into view under the sparse moonlight allowed by the trees. Quincy crouched as he crossed the tree line onto the property and made his way to the back corner of the building. The smell of lake sediment and rotten vegetation hit him before he encountered the creature. Hunched over and making a wheezing sound, the thing turned to face him. He heard footsteps nearby and a man's voice shout.

"Come back out here!"

Quincy had no idea who was on the other side of the cabin, but he knew it was a man with a gun.

The creature slumped to the side of the cabin. Its features were hard to figure. The moonlight was shaded from this back half of the building.

Taking a step back, Quincy yelled, "Leilani?"

"Quincy?"

"Are you all right?"

"Yes."

"Stay put. The cops are coming."

"Who else is out there?" she asked.

The creature lunged at him. Quincy tripped as the thing's slick, webbed hands traced the front of his shirt before sliding down the front of his body and wrapping around his knees.

Maddox was out of time. His chest felt like it was filled with cement. The teens were alive. And he was pretty damn sure at least a few of his shots had hit that hideous thing. Light suddenly flooded the yard. Maddox fell to a knee at the corner of the cabin. He heard the boy's cries from around the corner. Maddox spat and made his final play. "Let's fucking finish this."

Rounding the corner with his gun aimed and ready, he was unprepared for what he saw.

CHAPTER 23

LEILANI MADE HER way from the fuse box she'd found in the closet near the front room and got the power on. She headed back toward where she'd heard Quincy calling her name. The ruin of her foot was temporarily forgotten as she heard someone gagging. Opening the back door to the cabin, she saw the creature on top of Quincy. Beneath the bright lights, its black, scaled backside flexed and relaxed. It didn't even bother turning when she shouted, "Get off him!"

"Back inside," a man said, his voice filtered through a layer of phlegm. She saw a tall, sickly-looking man holding a gun aimed right at the creature's back. Leilani stood in the doorway as the man brought the butt of the gun down on the back of the thing's head.

The monster swatted the tall man away, knocking him off his feet. Leilani caught a glimpse of Quincy. The lower half of his blue face was covered in blood. As he gasped for air, his eyes found hers.

Undeterred, the creature reattached itself to Quincy.

"Help him!" she screamed.

The man slumped forward and tried to get his feet under him, but faceplanted in the soil. He did not move again.

Quincy's left hand swatted at the creature's head, each swing growing slower and weaker as he fought. He was going to die if she didn't do something.

Ignoring her injuries, Leilani sprung from her good foot, tucking her knees up and landing with them square into the creature's back. She hit the ground, pain shooting through her foot and up her leg. But it worked. She'd knocked the lake monster from her friend and straight into the rock beside them. It fell next to her and did not move.

It wasn't enough, and she knew it. Rolling to her knees, she scoured her surroundings for a weapon—anything she could use to finish this thing. Quincy was shaking his head from side to side and pawing at his mouth, making awful sucking noises as he tried to catch his breath. Turning her head toward the woods, Leilani spotted a wooden stick, maybe two and a half to three feet in length, sticking up from the ground and leaning to the side. A pink ribbon was wrapped around the end of it. It was a property marker, and she knew they usually ended in a point.

Like a stake.

She hadn't seen many horror movies in her life, but she knew how you killed vampires. Why wouldn't it work with lake monsters, too?

The marker was at least ten paces into the trees. She would need to hurry before the creature could retaliate against her or reattach itself to Quincy. Already the monster was stirring.

Quincy's mind raced with visions of his demise.

I'm still . . . breathing . . . .

A series of outdoor floodlights he never knew were still in working order had brought the Nietzsche Anathema into full grotesque view. Its beady black orbs had peered through his soul and into his stammering heart.

And now, as Quincy struggled against his contaminated lungs, the creature began to rise. He could see her—the angel from his daydream, Leilani—hopping toward the woods on her one good foot. The Nietzsche Anathema gave Quincy a quick glance that sent a fresh icy current through the boy's insides before turning its attention back to Leilani and lumbering after her.

It was coming. She already knew she would not make it to the marker before it caught her and did its weird mouth-to-mouth attack on her. She had no other choice. Leilani tried to run, and regretted it instantly. The second her ruined foot hit the ground, she knew she was done. She felt the full fire of the dirty spike throbbing in her wound all over again. She screamed as her body folded over, dropping her shoulder-first into the forest floor. There came an audible *snap* in her collarbone, accompanied a sudden heat sensation beneath the flesh. Tears streaming down her tan cheeks, Leilani decided it was over.

Her last words were for Tina and Todd.

"I'm sorry."

CHAPTER 24

QUINCY'S LEGS WERE rubbery as he got to his feet. His lungs burned like the midnight sun in some horror film filled with vampires and werewolves. Fiery sensations crawled up his insides, through his scorched throat and into his mouth. Everything hurt, but he couldn't let the creature reach Leilani. One foot in front of the other, he pushed his pace until he was in a full sprint. Already sweating and panting as if he'd run the full mile for Mr. Shagory in Phys Ed, Quincy ran until his lungs were ready to explode through his chest and splatter the forest floor along with his heart and soul. The Nietzsche Anathema was in striking distance, hobbling along, closing in on Leilani as she continued to crawl away. It reached out for her legs.

Quincy shouted. *"Hey!"*

The creature stopped and turned.

Quincy reached down and cried out like a warrior in the Lord of the Rings movies he used to love watching with his dad. The scream tore from the bottom of his soul, and gave Quincy the strength to throw himself at the lake monster.

This was it. The moment that held their death or their future. Gritting her teeth, tasting the blood, sweat, and soil coalescing inside her mouth, Leilani growled her way to her good foot, and hopped to the target. Clenching the wooden post in her palms, she could hear Todd giving her hell over not wearing work gloves, telling her that she'd get a splinter. She indeed felt the bite of a sliver of wood, but heaved the stake from the ground and started back to save Quincy.

Voices in the distance shouted in the dark, but it was white noise to Leilani. Quincy struggled in the creature's scaly arms. Its mouth was inches from his own, and his face was red with exertion. She got as close as she could, the thigh muscle in her good leg crying out in pain. And as she prepped for the lunge, she said a prayer to the lord of the universe to give her this one thing. After all the bullshit of her life, her dad's death, her mother giving her up, one horrible 'home' after the next, the adults that never cared about her, the schools, the fucking system . . . Leilani put it all into this one moment, this one motion.

She launched herself in the air and toward the creature from the lake.

Quincy's arms were wet spaghetti; he couldn't hold the Nietzsche Anathema back any longer. He closed his eyes and clamped his mouth shut in hopes of keeping the thing's grotesque lips from his own. It's hook-like teeth closed in for another round.

The monster suddenly screeched in his face, the sound of excruciating agony. It was so loud Quincy was startled beneath it as the creature fell to its side, spasming and squealing. Quincy rolled away and sat up, staring at the amazing girl kneeling atop the monster. She looked like a tattered angel, a warrior who'd been through the gates of hell and back and had conquered her ultimate foe.

The creature's screams deteriorated to whimpers, and then to nothing as it ceased moving. Leilani's shoulders hitched. Tears streamed down her beautiful face. Quincy moved to her and wrapped her in his arms. They stayed that way, both shaking and shedding the misery and fear of the day. They were survivors.

Flashlights in the darkness cut through the dark spires and skeletal branches of the trees like long light sabers in a galaxy far, far away. Voices grew louder. Help was finally here.

EPILOGUE

HER HEART HAD never been so open. Leilani's walls had been battle-tested her entire life, and she was convinced that no one, let alone multiple someones, would help her tear them down. Todd and Tina rushed to Maine General Hospital in Augusta where Leilani was treated for multiple wounds. The foot did wind up getting infected, but the doctors had anticipated such. They pumped her full of antibiotics and held her for observation. Todd and Tina snagged a room at a nearby hotel and stayed with her until the infection cleared and she was released.

Quincy was not so lucky. He was the bravest boy Leilani had ever met, and she would give him anything he needed from now until forever if he asked. His mom had come up and stayed with him while his father took a truck driving job. She gave Leilani her cell number and kept her up to date on Quincy's condition over the next four weeks. His lungs had been severely damaged by whatever the thing by the lake had done to him, and he'd have permanent scars around his mouth, but the doctors told him those would fade over time. He eventually did get to go home with his mom in Sebago which was a little closer to where she lived in New Hampshire. His lung damage would never fully heal, but he would be a mostly healthy teenage boy going forward. No running track in his future, but he'd shown an interest in writing. Leilani asked if he'd ever write about the creature, and he said no. He wanted to write about adventure and mystery. He'd had enough of scary things.

The remains of Henry Owens were never found. His wife claimed complete ignorance and went on to run the Owens Corporation alone. Her private detective had seemingly disappeared into thin air, as well. The kids who were found that day claimed a man fitting Maddox's description had saved them from a lake monster. The official report to hit media was that Francis Owens, a Vietnam vet and former professional boxer, brother to the missing Henry Owens, had snapped and attempted to murder the young teens, frightening them in some elaborate disguise. Francis Owens was found dead in one of his own wartime traps around the lake.

Maddox's head broke the lake surface from below, his beady eyes taking in the nightlife. The creature had changed him. His new form promised a path unlike any he'd ever taken, and he looked forward to it.

Twin lights blossomed in the dark. Maddox watched the car headlights as the vehicle traced its way around Lakeside Road. If he could still make a smile with his mouth he would. Instead, he wiggled his fresh fangs and dived back into the depths of Owens Lake.

IN THE GLASTENBURY WOODS

TOM DEADY

AUGUST 1986

"SHOULDN'T WE BE in Massachusetts by now?"

I shifted my eyes to the rearview mirror, biting back a profanity-laden response. The day was slipping away, the shadows darkening, aided by the seemingly endless forest on both sides. I switched on the headlights. "Negativity and Hulkamania are two things that don't go together," I said. Mark Trentino leaned over from the back seat and raised a hand for a high-five. I slapped his palm, then punched the shoulder of the figure slumped in the passenger seat. "Wake up, asshole."

Pat Keary sat up, wiping a trail of drool from his chin. "What?"

"You're supposed to be navigating. Where the hell are we?"

Pat grabbed the map from his lap and flipped the overhead light on.

"Hey!" I shielded my eyes from the glare. "There's a flashlight in the glove box, use that, numbnuts." He reached up and switched off the light.

"Calm down, Dave," Pat mumbled, pulling out the small flashlight.

"Do you even know how to read that thing?"

Mark flipped me the bird without looking up from the map. "Are we still on Route Eleven?"

I peered through the gathering gloom looking for a sign. "We should be, I haven't turned since we got off the highway." We were on our way back from Toronto after seeing the Big Event. Junkyard Dog, Adrian Adonis, King Kong Bundy, Ricky Steamboat, and a bunch of other professional WWF wrestlers all fought on the same night. And the final match had featured Hulk Hogan versus Paul Orndorff. Hogan had won on a bullshit disqualification, but that was all right with me. My friends didn't know it, but the wrestling match wasn't the real reason I had gone. I patted my pocket for the hundredth time, making sure the picture was still there.

Still, it was a fitting road trip to end our last summer together. I would be attending Boston University the following week, and Mark was going to the University of Massachusetts in Amherst.

The Zoo, as it was affectionately known. In fact, we would be dropping him off there on our way home. Pat had enlisted in the army as soon as he turned eighteen and was heading to boot camp in October.

"Well," Pat said, tracing a finger on the map, "from Route Eleven we take Route Thirty, then when we hit Route Seven, go south and we'll eventually cross the Mass Pike. Right back on course."

"Let me see that," Mark said, gesturing from the back seat. Pat handed him the map and the flashlight and Mark traced the route. "Pat's right for a change, but, man, we'll be going straight through the asshole of nowhere."

"It's Vermont," I said, "the whole state is the middle of fucking nowhere."

Pat laughed. "Hey, if we're going to be off the highway for a while, we should grab a couple six-packs."

"Yeah," Mark said, "I have to take a piss anyway."

I looked at the gas gauge: still half a tank, but if we were going to be driving through the boonies, I'd feel better doing it with a full tank. "Sounds good, keep your eyes open for a gas station."

For the next few minutes, only Pat's attempts to find anything but static on the radio broke the silence. Finally, I spotted the sign for Route 7. The intersection was a mile away. Just beyond the sign sat a dimly lit gas station with a convenience store. Pulling into the parking lot, I said, "All right, ladies. I'll pump the gas if you grab the beer and the snacks."

Mark and Pat were both just eighteen but had fake IDs and looked older. I was only seventeen but could pass for fifteen if I had to. *Good thing the beer isn't up to me,* I thought, following the others into the store and digging out my wallet. If we'd made the trip a few weeks earlier, Pat and Mark could have bought alcohol legally, but Vermont had raised the drinking age to twenty-one that July.

"Evening, boys."

Mark and Pat nodded to the shop assistant and headed down the aisles while I approached the counter. "Evening," I replied. "How's it going?"

"Oh, pretty fair, I'd say," the man said with a grin.

He looked to be about sixty, rail-thin, with gray hair and a couple days of stubble on his face. He reminded me of someone, but I couldn't place who. He wore a tattered flannel shirt with the sleeves rolled up, showing off a US ARMY tattoo.

"Ex-soldier?"

The old man nodded. "Damn right. South Pacific during WWII." He reached into his shirt and pulled out his dog tags.

"I don't know how you guys did it," I said. "I can't even imagine what it must have been like."

"Wasn't a party, that's for sure."

"You must have seen a lot. Terrible things, I mean."

The others returned with two six-packs of Miller Lite and an armful of junk food.

The man jutted his chin at the beer. "You boys have IDs for that?"

"Yes, sir," Pat said, reaching for his wallet.

The man waved him off. "I'm just messing around. Just don't go getting yourselves killed or I'll feel guilty." They all laughed, then the man turned back to me, his face hardening. "Yeah, I seen some bad things overseas, but I've seen worse since I've been back. Since I moved up here, anyway." He began tallying up the goods.

"Oh," I said, "I'm going to put ten dollars in on Pump Three."

The man nodded, finally looking up. "Comes to twenty-seven fifty with the gas."

The boys each threw ten dollars on the counter and the man handed over the change and bagged up the beer and the snacks.

"So, what kind of things have you seen up here?" I asked. I wasn't usually one for small talk, but there was something startling in the man's eyes that made me curious.

"Hey, was it Champ?" Mark said excitedly, "that Loch Ness Monster thing up in Burlington?" my friend loved local folklore, the weirder the better.

The old man sneered. "That's nothing but tourist bullshit."

I didn't like his tone, it was angrier than it should have been.

"I'm talking real stuff," he went on. History."

"You can't leave us hanging," I said, leaning on the counter. "What kind of stuff?"

Pat grabbed the bags. "Hey, can you turn the pump on? Dave, I'll go gas up while you listen to your campfire stories." He gave a half-wave at the old man. "Thanks, have a good night."

The old man watched him go. I shook my head. Pat was the polar opposite of Mark. If he couldn't see it, couldn't touch it, he didn't believe it existed. Folklore and local mysteries were something he scoffed at.

"Sorry about him," I said. "We really want to hear."

The man punched in the numbers to activate the pump. "All right, then. But if you can't sleep tonight, don't go blaming old Ray." He smiled when he spoke, but his eyes remained hard. "Where you headed, anyway?"

"Amherst, Mass," I said.

The man frowned, his bushy eyebrows almost meeting in the middle. "You're heading down Route Seven, then?" He licked his lips and swallowed, making his prominent Adam's Apple bob up and down.

"That's right," Mark said cautiously. "Is something wrong?"

Something cold settled on the back of my neck. I fell somewhere between Mark and Pat in terms of the local legends and campfire stories. But I wasn't sure I wanted to hear what the old man had to say.

"Route Seven takes you through Glastenbury and Lone Tree, you know that, right?"

He was staring at Mark, but there was an unsettling emptiness in his eyes. "Listen," I said, "what are you getting at?"

The muscles in the old man's jaw flexed as he stared out of the window behind us. I swear I heard his teeth grinding. "Never mind, you boys should probably get on the road. It's about an hour to the Massachusetts border."

"Come on, man. You said it was history. What gives?" Mark's tone wasn't angry, more perplexed.

I watched the man carefully, the coldness on my neck spreading down my back like ice water. One of the man's eyes began to twitch. His indecision was obvious. *Something is off,* I thought, not knowing if it was the story he was about to tell or the old guy himself. Finally, he gave a long sigh and his shoulders slumped. He reached into the pocket of his flannel and pulled out a rumpled pack of Camels, lighting one with a wooden match he had tucked behind his ear. He took an aggressive puff, slowly letting it out. My eyes flicked to the "No Smoking" sign behind the counter, but he ignored me.

"A lot of bad things happen in Glastenbury," the old man continued, in a cautious, smoky voice. "People see things in the sky. And there's other weird stuff. It goes all the way back to when

Native Americans were the only inhabitants. They wouldn't live in that part of the forest, they only used it to bury their dead. Then there's this giant cairn, you know, a pile of rocks? But it's up near the summit of a mountain where there ain't no rocks. So why would anybody lug all those rocks up there just to build a cairn? Mostly, people have a habit of going missing, never being seen again."

"It sounds kind of like the Bermuda Triangle, where all those planes and ships disappeared." Mark's eyes were wide. He and I had watched a documentary on the Bermuda Triangle when we were in middle school and Mark had become obsessed with it for a while.

The old man nodded. "That's right. Only it's people disappearing, hikers and such, instead of planes and boats. And there's another thing . . . people have reported seeing a creature—"

"Bigfoot?"

Mark was practically salivating. I touched his arm and tried to give him a look to calm him down. Most likely the old guy was just pulling our leg. Then I looked at the man again and realized I was wrong. This guy believed every word he was telling us. It was written all over his face, especially in his eyes. They looked . . . afraid. No . . . *haunted.*

"You've seen it," I said. "You've seen something." It wasn't a question.

The man swallowed, making his Adam's Apple dance again. "It's not Bigfoot, least not the way I've heard it described, and what I saw was different. It was . . . " He paused, staring off at nothing, at least nothing I could see. "It was more like a person, but covered in coarse hair, or fur. But not quite like Bigfoot. Bigfoot is supposed to look more like ape-like." He shook his head, his eyes returning to normal. "I'm not explaining it proper."

"And you saw this . . . thing?"

"Sure did, right down off Route Seven, the way you boys are headed." He jerked his hand, not noticing his cigarette had burned all the way down while he'd been talking. He snuffed it out in an ashtray he'd pulled from under the counter. "Was fishing by Black Brook. It was still fairly early in the evening, but it gets dark real quick in the forest. And those are some dense woods down there. I was just packing up, making sure I had enough time to hike out before full dark, when I heard rustling in the underbrush. I stayed still, quiet, and watched a good-sized buck come over to the brook to drink. It was about fifty yards upstream."

He paused, his eyes doing that faraway thing again. He pulled out his pack of Camels, looked at them, then returned them to his pocket. "I went back to packing up my gear, trying to be quiet so's not to disturb the deer. I love fishing but was never a hunter. Anyway, I heard thrashing and splashing. I thought the deer had been spooked and was running across the stream, but when I looked . . . "

"What?" Mark looked as though he were about to explode.

"I saw the creature, animal . . . whatever it was. It was having at the deer, ripping it apart with its bare hands . . . or claws, and its teeth. I'd never seen nothing like it, and haven't since. I couldn't pull my eyes away. That . . . thing dismembered the deer in less than five minutes. It would tear a leg off, eat some of it, then toss it aside and rip another piece off the poor thing. When parts of the deer started floating by me in the creek, I bolted. Ran out of those woods like Old Scratch himself was chasing me, kept running right across Route Seven - I live right by the entrance to the trail on the southbound side - almost got plugged by an eighteen-wheeler. Left everything there, all my fishing gear, and never went back for it. Ain't never gone back into those woods since."

Nobody spoke for a minute. The only sound was the insectile buzzing of one of the flickering fluorescent lights. If this was just a campfire story, the old guy should be in Hollywood. Nobody could act as terrified as he looked.

"Last thing I heard about was three hunters going in—"

The bell above the door jingled and I looked up to see a police officer walk in, smiling.

"Evening, Ray. You're not telling these boys any of your stories, I hope."

The old man—Ray's—face collapsed. He looked like the proverbial kid with his hand in the cookie jar. "No, just ringing them up, is all."

The cop looked at the counter, empty except for the ashtray.

He said something that sounded like *fucking around again* but I couldn't be sure.

"Don't you boys worry about old Ray here. Nothing up in those woods but deer and maybe a few coyotes. No crazy murderer, no little green men, and no Bigfoot."

Ray threw his shoulders back, cheeks flushed. "What about those three hunters a few years back?"

The cop flicked his hand dismissively like he was brushing dirt off an imaginary table. "They were from Massachusetts, probably shot their own dicks off and died from exposure."

"We're from Massachusetts," I said.

The cop shrugged. "Don't shoot your dick off or sleep up in the mountains without the right gear, and you'll be fine."

"I assume they never found the hunters?" Mark asked, eyeballing the cop.

"They did not," said Ray in a clipped tone.

"How do you explain *that*, officer?" Mark said pointedly.

I threw him a look, wishing he would change his tone. Not a good idea to piss off a cop in the middle of nowhere. Especially when you're underage and have beer in your car. "Chill out, Mark. It's just stories. I bet every small town in the mountains has them."

The cop pointed at me and winked. "You should listen to this guy, sounds like he's got half a lick of sense in him."

I watched the cop carefully. Something wasn't right but I couldn't put my finger on it.

Ray bristled but said nothing. Maybe he was thinking about selling beer to underage kids and had decided to hold his tongue.

"Anyway," I said, "we've still got a long ride ahead of us. Have a good night, Ray." I nodded to the cop. "Officer."

"Safe travels, boys," the cop said cheerily.

"Be careful up there." I shivered at Ray's tone. It was full of dread—and there was stark terror on his face.

"Mark," I said, leaning close as we crossed the parking lot, "when we get to the car, grab the beer and put it in the trunk."

Mark nodded. "Yeah, I was thinking the same thing, that cop freaked me out a little."

"More than a little," I replied.

Pat was already halfway through a bag of Doritos when we reached the car, but luckily he hadn't opened the beer. Mark went around to the other side and asked Pat for the bag of beer.

"Your wish is my command," he said, handing over the bag without question.

I grabbed the keys from the front seat where Pat had tossed them, and met Mark at the trunk. Quickly, we put the beer in, and for good measure, covered it with an old blanket.

"Let's get out of here," Mark said, glancing back at the store. I did the same, immediately regretting it. The cop was staring out the window at us. He raised his hand in a mock salute. We waved back, then got in the car. I started the engine and pulled out of the parking lot cautiously.

"Is he still watching?" I didn't want to take my eyes off the road for even a split second.

"Nope," Mark replied. I exhaled, not realizing I'd been holding my breath. "Now he's on his way to his car," Mark continued.

"What's the big deal?" Pat's question came crunching through a mouthful of chips.

I flipped my gaze back and forth between the road and the rear-view mirror so fast I was making myself dizzy.

"Did you not see the cop go into the store right after you went out?" Mark sounded exasperated.

"So?" Pat crunched.

"So we're eighteen and we have beer, jackass. The cop was acting really weird, too. Like he was on drugs." Mark was sounding panicky.

"Think he'll share?" Pat laughed at his own joke.

"Sure," Mark said, "right before he locks us up for the night."

Pat sat up straight and turned to look out the rear window. "Are you guys serious? I thought you were in there trading ghost stories with the old guy from Friday the Thirteenth."

I barked out a laugh despite my nervousness. "Crazy Ralph!" Now that Pat had mentioned it, that's who the guy reminded me of. Right down to the doom-and-gloom warnings. *And look what happened to those kids*, I thought. "We were," I said, "then that cop came in and Ray—the old guy—kind of shut up."

"Whatever," Pat said, "the beer's in the trunk and if you don't drive like an asshole, we have nothing to worry about."

I nodded but couldn't help from glancing in the rear-view mirror. Something had really seemed off about the whole encounter, but mostly it was the strange behavior of the cop. He'd acted bizarrely cheerful, yet Ray had seemed almost afraid of him. I tried to shake it off but the feeling was clinging to me like an unwelcome smell. I considered turning around and going back to the highway, but decided I was just being paranoid.

The headlights caught the sign for the Route Seven junction, and I breathed a sigh of relief. Still no car coming behind me. I *was* being paranoid. Once on Route Seven, I calmed down, as if that one turn had put a barrier between us and the oddball cop. I saw a sign for Sunderland but there didn't look to be much there. Still, I wished we'd waited until we'd got there to stop for gas and beer.

Once out of town limits, the thick forest encroached on both sides of the road. Towering white pines with thick undergrowth created the illusion of an impenetrable green wall. Occasional flashes of light indicated an isolated house here and there, but those disappeared altogether after a few miles. Then, it was only us and the deep woods. Nothing but darkness on all sides.

A pair of headlights brightened the rear-view mirror, and when I noticed how quickly the vehicle was approaching, my gut tightened. *Here we go,* I thought. A moment later, the bubble lights came on. "Here he comes," I announced.

Pat had been dozing in the passenger seat but sat up and checked behind him. "Shit, you guys weren't kidding."

I caught Mark's eyes in the mirror. He looked scared. I took my foot off the gas and put my right blinker on, pulling over to the shoulder. Less than a minute later, the police car whipped by, without even slowing down.

"Huh," I said, "I guess it was just a coincidence."

Pat scowled. "Was it even the same cop?"

"I think it was," Mark said, "but I can't be sure."

I took a deep breath and let it out slowly. The taillights of the cruiser had disappeared; only the ghostly reflection of the red-and-blues reflected off the trees in the distance. I shut off the blinker and pulled back onto Route Seven, driving slower. I just wanted to get to Massachusetts and find a place to crash for the night. All the fun was being sucked out of the trip.

"Being with you guys is like road-tripping with the Golden Girls," Pat said, again laughing at his own wit.

"Oh, hey, Pat," Mark said suddenly, "I forgot to tell you."

"Yeah, what?"

Mark flipped both middle fingers. "To go fuck yourself."

"I would if your mother hadn't worn me out," Pat replied, never missing a beat.

They both laughed. I smiled, too, still carefully watching the road ahead.

When I rounded a slight bend in the road a few minutes later, I wasn't surprised to see the bubble lights up ahead.

Pat craned his neck. "Must be an accident."

"I can't see past the lights," Mark said.

We were still a couple miles away from the scene when a weird feeling came over me. Something was gnawing at me, and even though I couldn't figure out what it was, it scared me. "Do you think we should turn around? Go back to the highway?" I hated that my voice had come out so high-pitched and full of fear.

"Fuck that," Pat crowed. "You're not serious? It'll add an hour just to get us back where we started."

"I don't know, Pat," Mark said, leaning forward, "if the accident's bad enough, we might be sitting here for longer than that waiting for them to clear it."

"You don't know that," Pat said incredulously. "What the fuck is wrong with you two?"

We drew closer to the lights and I eased back on the gas pedal. We were less than a mile away, now. I again found Mark's eyes in the rear-view. *He feels it, too.*

"You didn't see that cop, man," Mark said, "it was—"

"Fuck!" I slammed on the brakes and swerved to the side of the road. Luckily, I hadn't been going very fast and was able to avoid the cop with the flashlight, who seemed to have come out of nowhere.

"What the hell," Pat said, "that's not . . . "

"Evenin', boys," the cop said, shining his flashlight into the window. He shone the beam around the car. "We meet again." He pointed the beam up at his face, throwing it into a horrifying mix of light and shadow, like a camp counselor about to tell a scary story.

I bit back a gasp, then the situation hit me, or rather, the *possibilities* of the situation. Like how close I had come to either hitting the cop or veering off into the trees. "What the hell are you doing out in the middle of the road in the pitch black? Are you insane?" The cop smiled, still holding the light that way, and I shrunk away from him. "Sorry," I said, "I'm a little freaked out."

"Well, that makes two of us, chum. After all, I'm the one that almost ended up as your new hood ornament."

I forced a laugh as I fought back panic. "Okay, can we get by or should we turn around?"

"Neither," the cop said.

He finally lowered the light, getting rid of that ghastly countenance. His single-word answer chilled me. *This is where he pulls his gun,* I thought.

"You can't get by. Eighteen-wheeler jack-knifed. Both lanes completely blocked. A real clusterfuck. Tow-truck guys will be fudgelling around for hours."

That was the word he'd used back at the store. Not "fucking around," he'd said "fudgelling around" when referring to Ray. "So . . . "

"Well," he said, dragging the word out too far, "you *could* turn around, I suppose. But if you're heading to Massachusetts . . . " He shook his head as if it were the saddest thing he'd ever heard.

"We're not getting any younger here," Pat said, leaning over from the passenger side. The cop's eyes flashed, cold and hard. "Sir," Pat added shakily.

He gave Pat a smug look that bordered on sinister. To me, that look said *Watch your mouth, kid. I'm holding all the cards here. And I'm the one with the gun.* I braced myself against a shiver.

"Anyhoo," the cop continued, still eyeing Pat, "if I were all hot and bothered to get to Burlington and a truck driver all hopped on black beauties flipped his rig in my way, here's what I'd do." He paused. And the pause stretched uncomfortably as the cop stared past Pat, into the woods. I cleared my throat and the cop started, his focus coming back from wherever it had been. "I'd take the old Glastenbury Road," he said, gesturing up ahead. "It meanders a bit but eventually hits Lone Pine Road. You turn right and end up back on Route Seven, about two miles beyond this mess."

"Sounds great," Pat said, "thanks. The road is right up ahead?"

"Righty-o," the cop said, "I was just getting ready to set up the detour signs when you boys came along." He aimed his beam up ahead a bit, and sure enough, bright orange sawhorses lay unassembled on the gravel shoulder. Metallic "DETOUR" signs were piled next to them.

I relaxed when I realized the cop had a reason to be there and was actually setting up a detour. I'd been having some crazy thoughts about the cop and it was starting to look like it was all my paranoia. Sure, he was a bit weird, but not the homicidal lunatic I'd been building him up to be in my head. "That's great, officer," I said, trying to sound grateful even though the cop was still freaking me out. "Thanks for the help. That sounds like the best plan."

The cop stood and gave another of his two-finger salutes. "I'll walk up ahead to the road and shine my light for you." He pointed at me and winked. "Don't run me over, now."

I forced a smile and shook my head. "Thanks again," I called as the cop walked away.

"You're turning around, right?" Mark's voice was tight, his breathing too fast.

I turned in my seat to look at him. "No, we'll take the detour. The cop is a weirdo, but it looks legit." I studied my friend, not liking what I saw. Mark was beyond scared. He was bordering on panic. He looked ready to bolt, go running back the way we had come. "Mark, you okay?"

Mark shook his head, raising his hands in front of his face. They were shaking. Worse than that, his whole body was trembling, almost convulsing. A whistle cut the night and I looked up. The cop was waving his light. *The best thing is to get Mark away from the cop,* I thought. I pulled ahead, ignoring the keening sound that was coming from the back seat. Pat had turned around and was trying to calm him down. I tried to tune them both out. *Just get away from this guy.* I spotted the small road the cop was pointing his light toward and took the turn, giving the cop a final wave on the way by.

"Is he all right?"

Pat's voice was wrong. I realized he might be losing it, too. "Calm down, both of you," I said, with the sternest tone I could muster. "Let me get a little distance between us and that asshole cop, and we'll pull over and have a beer." I focused on the road. The asphalt was cracked and broken, more potholes than road. I maneuvered the vehicle carefully, not willing to risk blowing a tire. After a few hundred yards, I spied an opening where I could pull over. It was the site of an old house, now gone, taken back by nature. But what might have been the driveway was still clear enough to fit the car.

As soon as I killed the engine, Mark was out of the car, power walking up the dark road. "Mark, wait!" I flipped the keys to Pat. "Grab a six-pack out of the trunk and come find us." I jogged up the road after Mark, calling his name.

The darkness was impenetrable. The thick fir trees on either side reached out for each other, forming a canopy over the narrow road. *I should have grabbed the flashlight,* I thought. I stopped running, listening for Mark's footsteps up ahead. The symphony of the forest was too loud. Crickets, peepers, and owls drowned my chance of hearing anything. It was creepy as fuck. Something crashed through the brush to my left. *Has Mark gone off the road?* "Mark! Mark, where are you?" I listened for a response but got none.

"Where is he?"

I almost screamed. "What the fuck, Pat?" He'd come up behind me, holding a six-pack. "I don't know," I said. "I heard something in the woods, but I don't think he'd leave the road."

Pat handed me the beer and cupped his hands around his mouth. "Marky! Come grab a beer, buddy!"

I twisted the cap off a bottle of beer and took a long pull. It was lukewarm but better than nothing. My throat had gone dry, all the uneasiness from talking to the cop was creeping back, like an unwanted tide. All this for a last-hurrah road trip? I touched my pocket again. The signed picture of Hulk Hogan was still there. No, I thought, not just a road trip. I suddenly missed my little brother. Couldn't wait to hand him the picture, see his eyes light up. To see him showing some life for a change—

"Where the fuck did he go?" Pat muttered, grabbing a beer from the carrier.

"Maybe we should go back and get the car?" I glanced around, the darkness pressing from all sides.

"Yeah," Pat whispered. "Good idea."

We started walking. I was acutely aware of the oppressive darkness, certain that something was going to leap out from the trees. My irrational fear shifted gears as we approached the car. Now, I was sure the tires would all be slashed. When I was close enough to see the tires were fine, I became convinced the car wouldn't start. But when I turned the key, heart pounding, the engine started. "Jesus," I whispered.

"What's that?"

"Nothing," I replied. "Just the sound of me losing my mind."

I eased back onto the road, flipping on the high beams. I wanted to step on the gas, find Mark, and get the hell out of the woods. They were freaking me out worse than the crazy cop. But I managed to keep a tenuous grip on my panic and made sure not to go above ten miles per hour. The pretense of this being a paved road had given up, I was now on a rutted dirt road littered with years-old rotting leaves from the deciduous trees that battled for space among the pines. We drove in silence, each staring anxiously through the windshield for any flash of color in the dark to indicate

Mark was up ahead. An old song lyric rattled in my head, something about the minutes turning to hours. I was certain we were not going to find him. At least not alive.

"There!" Pat shouted, pointing.

I squinted, and sure enough, was able to spot a figure running in the distance. I realized it was running *toward* the car, not away, and this sent fresh terror running through me. *What is he running away from?* Without thinking, I sped up, gripped by the vision of Mark being snatched by something in the woods before we could reach him.

I glanced at the speedometer—twenty miles per hour was reckless on this road. I had just eased off the gas when the car suddenly swerved. I grasped the wheel for dear life, turning into the skid. The car shuddered to a stop.

"What the fuck?" I heard Pat, felt his eyes on me, but didn't turn. I couldn't. Couldn't pull my hands from their death grip on the wheel. Couldn't move. "Dave?" A hand touched my shoulder. I recoiled, thankful my paralysis was broken.

"Let's go," I said, opening the door and stepping out into the night. Mark was just reaching the car, wild-eyed and out of breath. Pat and I grabbed him to check if he was hurt. There were no apparent injuries, but Mark was out of his mind. He was mumbling something I couldn't make out. He flailed to get out of our grasp, shoving us both away with adrenaline-fueled strength, and ran past the car, back the way we'd come. Pat and I turned to follow, when Mark's scream ripped through the night.

When we found him he was on his back, grabbing at his left foot. I was about to take a step toward him when Pat grabbed my arm, pulling me back. "Watch it," he said, pointing at the ground. In the eerie red light thrown from the car's taillights, I saw what he was pointing at, and was struck with debilitating dread. It was worse than panic, worse than terror, it was the fear—the *knowledge*—that I would not live through the night. On the ground, spread from one side of the road to the other, was a row of deadly-looking spikes. "That's tack strip, or something like that," Pat said, shaking. "Cops use it—" He stopped, the realization hitting him. "Oh, fuck."

I pulled out of his grasp, careful to step over the hazard, and knelt next to Mark. I pushed his hand away and untied his sneaker, pulling it off as gently as I could, then carefully removed the sock.

"Pat, go grab the flashlight out of the glove box. And there's some first-aid kit in there, I think."

"Mark," I said, lie flat, your foot's bleeding pretty good, I'm going to keep it elevated until I can get a better look at it." Mark did as I asked, his face tightening into a grim mask of pain. I pressed his bloody sock to the wounds, then looked again at the spikes. They were each at least three inches long, and more than one had gotten him.

Pat returned with the flashlight and pointed it at Mark's foot. He handed me the zip-lock bag that contained the first-aid stuff.

I dumped out the bag and stuffed it in my pocket. "What've we got?" I asked.

Pat rummaged through the contents. "Band-Aids, gauze, medical tape, and antiseptic cream."

"Okay," I said, trying to keep my breathing under control. Having something to focus on helped keep the panic at bay. "I'm going to wipe away as much of the blood as I can. Have the cream ready. I'll smear it on as best as I can, then tape the gauze over it. The band-aids are useless."

"It's that bad?" Mark's voice was reed-thin, his eyes clamped shut.

"It's chewed up pretty good, buddy, but we'll get you fixed up. We're almost to Bennington, there'll be a hospital there. They'll be able to stitch it up in no time."

Talking about hospitals brought images of Bennie, stick thin and bald in his hospital room. I pushed them away.

"What the fuck did I step on?"

I didn't answer. "Get ready, I'm going to clear away the blood now. I'll try not to hurt you." What I really meant was *this is going to hurt like a bitch, so grit your teeth and don't fucking kick me.* I pulled the sock away - it was already soaked through - and did my best to clear the blood to see the wounds. Mark screamed and jerked, trying to pull his leg away, but I was ready for him.

"Fuck," Pat said, almost reverently, and the light dropped slightly when he saw the excoriated foot.

"Hold still!" I snapped, still wiping. "Okay, give me the cream. Pat tried to hand me the tube but I pushed it away. "Just squeeze as much as you can into my hand." I felt my palm fill with the cold gel.

"Okay, that's it," Pat said, breathing as though he'd just run the hundred-yard dash instead of squeezing a tube.

I smeared the cream on Mark's foot, my stomach lurching when flaps of skin moved under my hand. He groaned but held his foot still. "Gauze," I barked, feeling like one of the doctors on *St. Elsewhere* asking a nurse to hand over a dressing. I wrapped the gauze tightly around Mark's foot, knowing it was going to be a bitch to get off. But that wasn't my problem, some emergency room intern could deal with that. "Tape," I said, but Pat was ready for me this time, already handing me the end of the medical tape.

I paused and looked around. We were being watched. My spine turned to an icy steel rod as I searched the sides of the road for . . . for what? A pair of glowing eyes? The crazy cop?

"Dave? What are you—"

"Nothing." I wrapped the tape around the foot until the small metal roll was empty. "Okay," I said, "that'll have to do. I'm going to unlace your sneaker and see if it'll fit over the bandage."

I eased Mark's foot down so the heel rested on the ground, then loosened the laces on the sneaker. I turned it over before trying to slip it back on, cringing at the three gaping holes and the shredded rubber. *The spikes must be serrated or something.* I shivered, then slipped the sneaker on. It barely went over the bandage but it didn't matter; Mark wasn't going to be doing any walking on it. I tied it just tight enough to keep it from falling off, then got to my feet. "Pat, give me a hand."

We crouched on either side of Mark. "Can you sit up?" He did and threw an arm over each of our shoulders. "Use your left foot to help you stand, no weight on the right, understand?" Mark nodded. "One, two, three!" We stood, pulling him to his feet. *Or,* I thought, *his foot.*

Mark let out a small cry, but that was all. "Okay, okay," he said, "let's get out of—" He finally noticed the car, sitting on four flat tires. "Oh, no. Nononono . . . " He began sobbing, his weight shifting awkwardly as his body trembled.

"Mark, stay with us. We're getting out of here." Mark continued sobbing, babbling incoherently as he did. I started walking toward the car. Mark hopped to keep pace. *At least he isn't completely catatonic,* I thought. I stopped in front of the row of tack strip. "One big step when I say so, okay, Mark?" His sobs had subsided into a hopeless sniveling, but he nodded. "Now," I said, taking an exaggerated step over the obstacle, watching to make sure he cleared it. We got him to the car and helped him into the back seat.

"What are we going to do?" Pat's face was hidden in the shadow thrown by the car's dome light. He looked old. And very, very afraid.

"Just I like I said, we're getting out of here. Get in, I'll be right there." I took the flashlight and followed the row of tack strip to the side of the road. The end of the strip was anchored in the dirt with what seemed to be a tent stake. Grabbing it carefully between the spikes, I yanked the stake up, surprised at how easily it came out of the dirt. I walked to the other side of the road, dragging the menacing row of spikes with me. I stepped into the woods to make sure the hazard was completely off the road, then started back to the car.

I stopped when an animal's howl split the night. It sounded close. As it trailed off to nothing, I took a step forward, then stopped, sensing something was wrong before realizing what it was. The woods had gone silent. Not quiet; completely and utterly silent. No rustling in the underbrush, no owls, no frogs, no crickets. It was an alien silence, unnatural. I tried to swallow but my throat had gone all sandpapery. *I need to get the fuck out of here.* I hustled back to the car, closed the door, and let out a deep breath.

"Lock the doors," Mark said from the back seat. "Oh Jesus-god, lock the doors and get us out of here."

"What—" I couldn't finish my question before Mark was screaming at me.

"There's something in the woods! That's why I was running back . . . oh god, drive!"

I didn't want to hear anymore. I shifted the car into drive and began a clumsy three-point turn on the rims and the shredded rubber of the tires. I had no idea how far I could drive like that, but I was sure as hell going to find out. The steering wheel jerked madly in my grip and the car shifted back and forth on its own as the remains of the tires were flayed by the rims. *Soon enough,* I knew, *it'll be metal to dirt, all the rubber gone*. I didn't give a shit.

"It's out there. I saw it. That old guy, Ray—"

"Shut up!" Pat's voice was raw with panic. "Just shut the fuck up!"

I gritted my teeth, focused on keeping the herky-jerky movements of the car from pulling us off the road completely. I ignored the bickering, clinging tenuously to my sanity. T*his is what it must feel like just before a person goes batshit crazy*. An earth-shattering baying surrounded the car. I couldn't tell where it had come from, only that it was closer than before.

"It's going to get us!" Mark thrashed in the back seat, trying to sit up.

The driving was painfully slow and even more unbearable with Mark jabbering and Pat screaming at him to shut up. A loud *POP* quieted everyone and we watched one side of the road go dark.

"What was—"

POP!

Complete darkness. I hit the brakes, bringing the car to a bumpy halt. Pat didn't need his question answered, it was obvious. Both headlights had been shot out.

"What's going on? Why did we stop?" asked Mark.

I sighed hopelessly. "Headlights are out," I said.

"What? Why?"

Another sound, this time more of a loud metallic *PING*, followed by the hiss of steam. The radiator was punctured. I sat waiting for the next shot. *Would it hit one of us? Were we next?* The moment stretched, the silence broken only by Mark's moans and Pat's heavy breathing.

"We're going to have to walk. We'll take turns helping you," I said to the mirror.

"Yeah," Pat said, "we can find a makeshift crutch or cane in the woods . . . " He stopped and I watched a shiver ripple through him.

The thought of going into the woods did the same to me. I switched off the ignition. "Anything you want from the trunk?" We each had a duffel bag for the weekend but there was nothing in mine I couldn't replace. The only thing I wanted from the trunk was the tire iron. It was the closest thing we had to a weapon.

Pat and Mark didn't want anything either. "Wait here a minute." I got out of the car and walked stiffly to the trunk, expecting a bullet to rip through me with each step. Then I realized I hadn't heard any gunshots, only the strange popping sound. I opened the trunk and shone the flashlight in, finding the tire iron. I pulled it out and hefted it, liking the weight of it in my hand. It would be no use against a gun, or whatever the cop had used to shoot out the headlights, but it would come in handy in close quarters.

I circled back to the passenger side. "Let's go."

Pat got out of the car, his head on a swivel as if there was something to see. The darkness was its own entity. It was utterly complete without even the red glow of the taillights to make a dent in it. Pat and I helped Mark out of the back seat. He leaned against the car while Pat took the flashlight and searched the edge of the woods for a decent-sized limb that Mark could use as a crutch.

I listened carefully for any movement in the woods but it was preternaturally quiet. The sounds of the night creatures had not resumed since the howls. Only Pat's rustling and the occasional ting of the cooling engine assured me I hadn't completely lost my sense of hearing. The air was still and warm, the day's humidity had lessened but had not completely disappeared. The sharp, sweet aroma of pine surrounded me. An errant breeze, barely perceptible, cooled my skin. On it wafted a new scent, something primal and musky. *Unclean,* I thought.

Pat stumbled out of the woods with a tree limb that had a branch sticking out at a right angle. It looked like the perfect size to use as a crutch if Mark wedged the smaller branch in his armpit. It would make this trek much easier if we didn't have to half-carry him. It would also make defending ourselves easier.

Mark tried it out, limping back and forth along the road. "This'll work," he said, his voice both thick and scratchy from all the crying and yelling. He cleared his throat, then hopped closer. "Are you ready to listen to what I saw?" He leveled his gaze at Pat. "I'd rather you know before we head out. Just in case . . . "

I *wasn't* ready to listen. Didn't want to know anything about whatever it was that had set Mark into such an irrational state. But if we were going to have any chance of getting out of this, I *had* to know. "Go ahead," I said. "No interruptions, Pat. Let him tell it. All the way through.

Pat saw something on my face that subdued any potential argument. He nodded and turned to Mark.

"When I left the car, I was having a panic attack. Walking around helps, you know, so I don't feel trapped. And I need to be alone . . . it's embarrassing." He was looking at the ground. "Another one of those howls came from the woods but it was impossible to tell which direction it came from." Mark jerked his head up, then went on. "Anyway, I don't know how long I'd been walking . . . time gets kind of weird when I'm like that. I was starting to calm down. The fact that it was dumb of me to run away was starting to make sense, and with that came . . . "

I put a hand on his shoulder. "It's okay, Mark. It's okay."

Mark nodded. "When I start to feel rational again after one of these, the next feeling is always humiliation. Like, how can I go back and face my two best friends after wigging out like that?" He took a deep breath and let it out. "Anyway, I'd been standing there for a few minutes, completely still, and I couldn't see my hand in front of my face it was so dark." He made a sound that might have been a laugh. "You know how people say that? I tried it. I actually couldn't see my hand in front of my face. I almost started to panic again, thinking I'd gone blind.

"I was about to turn around when I heard something in the woods, just off the road a little ahead of me. I stared at the spot where the sound had come from and I guess my eyes began to adjust. I could see a shape, just, like, a different shade of black against the shadows of the woods. It moved and I could see it coming closer. Really slow, though. I felt like it was looking at me."

Another baying howl exploded, this time closer, and it seemed to have come from the direction they'd planned to take. *It makes sense, if he shot out our headlights, he had to be in front of us. But what's with the howling*, I wondered. "Mark," I said gently, "who was it? The cop?" In the darkness, I saw him cock his head, eyes narrowed.

"No, it wasn't the cop. I thought it was a person, but—"

"Oh, fuck this," Pat cried. "I'm not listening to this bullshit. Let's go."

I grabbed his arm as he started moving away. "We said we'd listen. Don't be a dick."

Pat pushed my hand away, stepping closer. "Are you fucking kidding? We're wasting time when we could be getting back to the main road." He shoved me back against the car. "And watch your mouth."

I straightened, catching my balance. I started forward, hands curling into fists, when Mark slammed an open palm onto my sternum. "Stop! Both of you!" He turned to Pat. "If you want to go running off, go ahead. But you should know there's something out there. You can hear it howling, for Christ's sake."

"It's a coyote or something, that's all," Pat scoffed.

"No," Mark said, shaking his head, "it's not. And it's not a wolf, or a bear, or a fucking lunatic cop."

"Then what is it?" Pat screamed.

"I'm trying to tell you," said Mark.

I tried to appeal to my friend. "Pat—"

"No," Pat said, "fuck this. I'm gone." He stepped away quickly before I could try to grab him again. He disappeared into the night, calling back, "I'll send someone to help when I get to the road. If the fucking boogeyman doesn't get you."

I stared into the darkness, which Pat had seemed to become a part of. I couldn't believe it. Part of me wanted to go after him and drag him back, the other part wanted him to come face-to-face with whatever was out there. I turned to Mark. "Carry on. What did you see?"

"Like I said, it looked like a person, but as it got closer, something was . . . off. He . . . it . . . was sort of hunched over, *loping* more than walking. I think I gasped, or made some kind of sound, because it stopped. It went into a crouch. I took a step backwards and it leaped to its feet and crossed the road to the woods on the other side. It was fast. *Too* fast. And when it passed by me . . . It wasn't human, Dave." He stopped, shaking his head. "That's not right, either. I don't know. It was mostly covered in hair, but it wasn't like Bigfoot or anything. Maybe it was my eyes playing tricks on me."

I thought about the howls. Could they have been from some near-human? Or were they just a wolf or a coyote, like Pat had said? "Okay, are you ready to go?"

"Do you believe me?" Mark's voice was small, childlike. A kid asking his parents if they believed the outlandish lie he'd just told them.

"I believe you saw something. To be honest, I'm glad it wasn't the cop. Come on." We started walking. I let Mark set the pace. It was slow-going with his hobbling on a homemade crutch. I kept the flashlight pointed just in front of his feet so he was sure to land with both the crutch and his good foot on level ground. We'd only gone a few steps when a scream ripped through the night, taking most of my composure with it. As gruesome and agonizing as the screech had been, there was no mistaking it. "That was Pat," I whispered.

"It got him. I tried to tell him, Dave. You heard me, I tried to warn him!" His voice held the same pitch and the same madness of a whistling tea kettle.

"Calm down," I hissed. "Keep your shit together." Mark didn't answer but I heard his ragged breathing and knew it was touch and go with him. I started forward again.

"Wh-what are you doing?"

"We're getting out of here," I said.

"We can't go that way. We *know* it's up there."

"And a little while ago it was further up the road ahead of us in the other direction. It can move faster than us in the woods." I paused, trying to hold it together. "We have no idea what's in that direction," I said, and pointed where we'd originally been driving, deeper into the woods. I turned, pointing where Pat had gone. "That way, we know how far it is back to Route Seven."

Mark sniffled, close to sobbing again. He nodded, and I clapped him on the shoulder. We started walking again. Other than an occasional howl, the woods remained silent.

"What's that?" Mark was gesturing to something in front of us.

I waved the light around until the beam caught a flash of metallic reflection. It was a sign: *Black Brook 2 miles*. I moved the light down and could barely make out a narrow trail leading off into the woods. It looked like a fairytale lane that led to a witch's house. I had to stop myself from looking for a trail of breadcrumbs. "Didn't Black Brook cross Route Seven on the map?"

Mark gazed upward, eyes closed. "Yeah," he said, nodding, as if seeing the map in his head, "if we'd driven a little further north, it would have crisscrossed Route Seven a couple times, kind of running parallel with it. Why?"

An idea was forming but I wasn't sure if it was brilliant or crazy. "You said that thing you saw was walking toward you, right?"

"Yeah, but—"

"But it didn't react until you moved? And made a sound?"

"Right?"

"What if it relies more on sound, and maybe smell, not sight?"

"You think it's blind?"

"No, no, not blind. If it was that thing and not the cop that took out the headlights, it can clearly see. But the car was lit up. Even after the headlights were out, the parking lights still gave it an easy target. It doesn't make sense that it didn't attack you."

"I still don't know what you're getting at," Mark said, exasperated.

I pointed to the narrow gap in the trees that led to Black Brook.

"If we can get to the water, the river might cover our sound. And we know it leads to Route Seven."

"So does this road," Mark whined.

"We're sitting ducks if we stay on the road, in either direction," I said. "It already got Pat. It could pick us off one by one. If we try the woods, we'll make too much noise and probably end up lost."

"I don't know . . . "

"Nobody is coming for us, Mark. Except maybe that cop. And he's not coming to help, we know that." I looked up and down the road, then back to the Black Brook trail. "I think if we can make the two miles to the water, it's our best chance."

Mark stared at the narrow opening.

I saw the concern on my friend's face and knew what he was thinking. *How rough does the trail get?* I shared the same concern, envisioning rocky ledges and dangerous hilly sections of the trail. *And what about when we reach the water?* If it came to it, I'd try carrying him fireman-style.

Finally, Mark heaved an exaggerated sigh. "Fine, we'll try it."

"Good," I said, relieved. There was no way I was staying on the road, but the idea of splitting up terrified me as well. "There's not enough room to walk side-by-side, at least not here. Can you manage the light and the crutch? If not, I'll have to go first."

"I think so," Mark said, sounding doubtful. "I'll try. If I can't manage, we'll switch."

"Sounds good," I said. "I'm ready whenever you are."

We started on the trail, Mark hobbling awkwardly while the flashlight's beam jerked wildly about, throwing the shadows into lunatic dances. For a time—had no concept of how long—we continued that way, making slow but steady progress. The trail widened eventually, and I was able to walk next to Mark, helping support him to give him a break from the crutch. I figured we must have traveled at least a mile, with no signs of whatever it was he had seen. The same thing that had probably killed Pat.

That's when the trail narrowed again, the soft footing of years' worth of pine needles turning into uneven, rocky terrain. We would have to go single-file again, and the crutch would be treacherous.

"What time do you think it is?" Mark was winded, but sounded the calmest he had been since everything had started going to shit.

"I have no idea," I said. "After midnight?" I realized with a hollow feeling in my chest that Pat had been the only one among us who'd worn a watch. I pushed the thought away. There would be time for grieving later. Maybe. What difference did it make what time it was, anyway? "Do you think you can manage?"

Mark nodded. "Not like there's an alternative," he said, without bitterness.

He sounded like the old Mark. I smiled and we forged ahead, more slowly than before. A couple of times the crutch slipped and he swayed on the brink of falling, but both times, I was close by and able to keep him upright. If we had to wade in the river, I wasn't sure I'd be able to keep my friend standing.

"Listen," Mark said, stopping abruptly.

I paused. I'd been so focused on watching his footing that I hadn't realized I could hear the gurgling of the river. I laughed and slapped Mark on the back. "Almost there, buddy, we're going to make it." I knew the river was only the first step in getting out of the mess we were in, but it was a first step I hadn't thought we'd ever get to.

We forged ahead, the bushes and trees on either side of the path seeming to try to foil our progress. Heavy branches and sneaky vines reached for us, twice almost taking Mark down. We pushed on, the sound of the river getting louder with each step. When we fought through a thick pine bough, I almost collapsed with relief at the sight before me. We'd made it. I surveyed the river in the direction of the highway. The moonlight was filtered through thickening clouds, but there was enough of it for me to see I'd made the right call. The water flowed with enough current to drown out the sounds of our traveling, but there didn't look to be a lot of rocks to contend with. The shallow edge of the water was lined with a gravel-like bed. Not bad at all for Mark to cope with. At least in this section. Whatever lay ahead, we'd deal with it when we had to.

The water was icy but we got used to it quickly. Mark did his best to keep his bad foot dry, but inevitably it would dip below the surface and he would gasp as the water stung his open wounds. I took the inside, contending with slightly rockier footing, but it was fairly easy going.

We walked in silence. I was unsure how long, exactly; the slow pace and the constant dread of something breaking out of the trees made estimating impossible. It might have been fifteen minutes but could just as easily been an hour. With each step, I steeled myself for the bloodcurdling howl, but it never came. *We're getting out of this,* I thought, almost giddily. I knew we weren't completely out of trouble when we made the highway, but I was confident we could get safely to Bennington, no matter how long it might take.

Thin clouds skated across the moon, throwing the river in and out of that eerie blue light. I listened more carefully when we were thrown into that deeper darkness, but the sounds of the forest seemed normal. Crickets, peepers, small creatures skittering through the underbrush, and the occasional owl or coyote. Everything I would have expected to hear before the woods were forever ruined for me. Ray's words echoed in my head, "*I've never gone back into those woods since.*"

My heart bouncing oddly in my chest, I faced what looked like an impenetrable wall of darkness ahead. Then I realized the river took a sharp bend. I *was*, in a way, staring into a wall of darkness: trees. Looking up at the sky, it was easier to follow the river's course by the gap in the trees on either side of it against the paler sky. We navigated the sharp bend, which turned out to be an s-curve, then we were back on a straight, heading directly toward the highway.

The clouds thinned, giving us an unobstructed view for what could have been miles, the river flowed so arrow-straight. I squinted, unable to believe what I thought I could see on the horizon.

"Is that the overpass?" Mark's voice was barely audible, stealing my thought.

"I think so," I replied, hearing the wonder in my own voice.

Without talking about doing it, we both picked up the pace. Suddenly, Mark stopped with a gasp.

"What is it? Your foot?"

"Look up ahead, maybe fifty yards, dead center in the river."

I squinted, mentally estimating fifty yards. My gaze tracked forward and back until I spotted what Mark had seen. My throat tightened, a burning sensation igniting in my gut. I thought I might lose control of my bladder. Something stood in the river. It had a vaguely human shape, but the dark and the distance made it impossible to tell. I watched for several minutes, frozen in place, barely breathing. The clouds continued their ceaseless journey across the sky, never thinning enough to give me a good look at it.

Then Mark breathed out what might have been a laugh. "I think it's a tree. It hasn't moved and it looks too . . . deformed to be a person or . . ."

He didn't have to explain what the 'or' was. I smiled in the dark. "I think you're right. I damn near pissed myself over a tree."

We started moving again, slower now. Just in case. When we were within thirty yards, I was sure Mark was right. It still hadn't moved and there were definitely strange angles, branches either broken or growing haphazardly before the tree was swept into the river.

We were within ten yards of it when the clouds parted, casting a silvery-blue glow on the ghastly scene. It was no tree. Nor was it the creature, but it was just as bad. Pat's body - what was left of it - was impaled on a branch that was wedged in the rocks of the river. One leg dangled loosely in the current, the other was gone. His right arm was twisted behind his neck, his left appeared to end at the elbow.

A high-pitched wail arose. I scanned the woods before realizing it was coming from Mark. My own breath was coming in short gasps. The cold river water seemed to spread up my legs, enveloping my entire body. I started trembling, every muscle quaking out of control. The horrible reality was too much for me. We hadn't outsmarted the creature, it had been toying with us. Letting us think we had a chance to escape; all the while it had gotten ahead of us and set up this ghastly tableau.

I turned to the sound of a splash, expecting the creature to be bounding across the river, but it was Mark. He'd toppled face-first into the water, his arms spread out next to him, motionless. *He must have passed out from fear,* I thought, not knowing if that was even possible. I lunged forward, grabbing him by an arm and the back of his shirt, turning him over quickly before he could inhale any water. Blood poured from Mark's eye. *Has he been shot?* I leaned closer, seeing something I couldn't make out beneath the blood. I reached out tentatively, touching the object to confirm it was as I thought. A rock was embedded in Mark's eye socket. A piece of the puzzle fell into place. It explained why they hadn't heard any gunshots when the headlights and radiator had been taken out. *A slingshot.*

I dragged Mark's limp body onto shore and into the underbrush. The entire left side of his face had begun to swell already, the skin so tight it threatened to split. I grabbed the sharp edges of the rock, preparing to pull it out. I gagged and released my grip, not wanting to do further damage as his body convulsed against the hideous act. *What if I make it worse by pulling it out? The bleeding has mostly stopped . . . could removing the rock reopen the wound?* I decided to leave it as it was.

I felt around Mark's throat for a pulse, not really sure what I was doing. Finally, beneath my blood-soaked fingers, I found it. Weak and erratic. *How much damage has the rock done? And what am I supposed to do now? Leave him behind, wounded and alone, or stay with him and wait until whatever is hunting us comes for me?*

As much as the decision tore at me—and I knew it always would, no matter what happened—I had to try to get help. And that meant leaving Mark behind. I dragged my friend deeper into the forest and positioned him in a copse of small conifers that formed a natural hiding spot. I did my best to leave him as comfortable as possible, setting the flashlight and the makeshift crutch within reach. I would keep the tire iron for my own protection.

With a final pat on the shoulder, I left Mark, creeping as silently as I could through the brush until I was back at the water's edge, feeling like the world's worst friend.

My theory about the creature not being able to see very well had been dead wrong. It had put a rock in Mark's eye from who knows how far away. And with what, a slingshot? Now, I was going to head in the direction the thing had last been.

I was on my hands and knees, still partially concealed in the bushes, when an idea struck me. It would be worse on every level than walking on the path or in the river, but it might give me a better chance. Any chance.

I pulled the picture out of my pocket, then remembered the first-aid kit that was really just a plastic bag. I pulled that out of my pocket and placed the picture inside, sealing it and hoping it would be watertight.

I lowered myself and army-crawled into the river. The cold water shocked me, taking my breath away. I'd gotten used to it on my legs, but fully submerged, it was going to be tough going. The rocks and the gravel on the riverbed, easy for walking, were cutting my hands and elbows as I pushed myself forward. I refused to look when I passed Pat's body.

I continued forward, the river's cold sucking my body heat away. I trembled from cold, fear, and exhaustion, teeth chattering, muscles growing sluggish. *I can't make it,* I thought, hot tears bursting from my eyes. I conjured up images of Pat's obscenely displayed corpse, of Mark's ruined face, anger urging me on. I clenched my teeth together to stop the chattering and pushed ahead, moving faster now. I knew the adrenaline rush would fade and needed to make as much progress as I could.

As I forged ahead, the events of the evening whipped through my brain, a film on a loop at fast-forward speed. I forced my overtaxed mind to slow down, to analyze everything that had taken place to get me to this point, crawling along the river trying to avoid a creature that had killed one of my friends and severely injured another.

It had all begun at the gas station, that much was clear. Or had it? If the cop was involved, a fact the tack-strip made pretty clear, could he have somehow orchestrated the traffic issue that had made us try the detour? I wasn't ready to rule anything out, but that seemed pretty farfetched. I went over the conversation at the gas station, searching my mind for something, anything that might give me an advantage. A way out.

The cold water was making my muscles stiff, sluggish. I was shivering uncontrollably but knew staying in the water was my best bet. Maybe my *only* bet. I focused on replaying the conversation with Ray, and finally it hit me.

"I bolted. Ran out of those woods like Old Scratch was chasing me, kept running right across Route Seven—I live right by the entrance to the trail on the northbound side—almost got plugged by an eighteen-wheeler."

I grinned through chattering teeth. I didn't have to get all the way to Bennington, just across Route 7 to find Ray's house. No doubt the old man had a small arsenal there. More importantly, a phone. The cavalry would be there in no time. *Fuck that crazy cop.* I slurped up some river water and began crawling faster, the glimmer of hope I'd been clinging to growing that much brighter.

Time became irrelevant as I scrabbled through the icy river. The thoughts that ricocheted in and out of my mind were as random as dice rolls. The Big Event—the reason I was crawling for my life in the middle of the Vermont woods—seemed as insignificant as middle school to a high schooler.

One image kept playing out in my head. In January of that year, the first civilian-manned space shuttle, the Challenger, had been launched. Seventy-three seconds after take-off, the shuttle had exploded, killing everyone on board, including New Hampshire school teacher Christa McAuliffe. The footage had been played over and over, never getting any easier to watch. *What if,* I wondered, *they hadn't been killed instantly? What would it feel like knowing your death was imminent?* I thought I knew the answer. President Reagan had addressed the nation, and a line from that speech was permanently etched in my memory: "We will never forget them, nor the last time we saw them, this morning, as they prepared for their journey and waved goodbye and slipped the surly bonds of earth to touch the face of God." I shivered, unsure whether it was due to the cold, or the power behind those words. I crawled on.

At some point I realized I was crying. If I didn't make it back, Bennie would never get the autographed Hulk Hogan picture. *For Bennie,* Hulk had written, *the toughest little Hulkamaniac out there.* "Fucking cancer, I muttered, shaking from the cold river water and the hot anger at whichever god had picked my little brother to inflict.

Some unknown time later, I looked ahead and realized how close I was to the overpass. A wave of emotion swelled in me. Relief, hope, giddiness, madness, or perhaps a combination. I wasn't sure. The lunatic thoughts, so clear and vivid, flickered in my brain. Next up, part of Robert Shaw's famous Jaws monologue. When it came, it ripped away the solace I'd felt at seeing the overpass just out of reach.

"At noon on the fifth day, a Lockheed Ventura swung in low and he spotted us, a young pilot, lot younger than Mr. Hooper here, anyway he spotted us and a few hours later a big ol' fat PBY come down and started to pick us up. You know that was the time I was most frightened. Waitin' for my turn."

What if it gets me now, I thought, and had to suppress a giggle. To laugh now would surely mean lunacy, wouldn't it? Next thought, a random song lyric from a hit song that year, Howard Jones' *No One Is To Blame.* This one wouldn't come clear, but it was something about being able to see the summit but not being able to reach it. The cold, slippery fingers of panic took hold and began to squeeze. I resisted the urge to get up and run, instead gulping in a breath and dunking my head underwater. When I emerged, the panic persisted, but had lessened.

I was close enough that I had to make a plan. Would that thing, that creature, follow me on Route 7, or would it retreat back into the woods? Getting from the river to the relative safety of the road was where I would be most vulnerable. I considered staying in the river until I was on the other side of Route 7, but the thought of being in that dark tunnel terrified me.

All thoughts stopped, as though a switch in my head had been flipped to 'off', when I saw the figure ahead. I stopped crawling, my only movements the shivers that wracked my body. It was just a shape, standing by the side of the river. I stared, trying to keep my breathing steady. I couldn't make out anything about the figure, it was little more than a darker shade of black against the horizon. I thought I could see the outline of something in its hand. A gun? Or a slingshot? The cop, or the creature? The lady or the tiger? "Fuck it," I muttered through numb lips. I tightened my grip on the tire iron and started crawling again.

The figure remained motionless. I was within thirty yards of it but still couldn't make out any features. I was sure the gurgling of the river covered any splashing sounds I was making, and I wanted to get as close as I could before standing. Five yards closer. The figure moved, its head jerking. *Is it looking in my direction?* Hot tears of frustration burned the backs of my eyes. I hadn't come this far to die within a few yards of freedom. I hadn't watched one friend die and another get mutilated, maybe killed as well, without living long enough to honor their memory. I needed to tell Pat's family what had happened. I had to save Mark, or be the one to tell his family of his bravery. Blinking back the tears, I rose from the water.

I began walking toward the figure. Not announcing my approach but not trying to be quiet, either. I stepped onto the bank and took long, quick strides, my muscles loosening with each step. I was within fifteen yards. I quickened my pace and started raising the tire iron. The figure made a sound, I was unsure if it was a gasp or a moan or a growl, but I charged. It raised whatever it was holding. I saw the flash before I heard the gunshot. *The cop,* I thought, not the creature after all.

Screams shattered the night, a piercing mix of anguish and rage. I waited for the explosion of pain . . . but it never came. I realized the screams were not my own. The shot had missed, or rather, had not been intended for me at all. I turned to see the target, but it was gone; there was nothing left but the howls of pain and the crashing of something heavy through the forest.

"Let's go, boy," a vaguely familiar voice called. "That might not be the only one of 'em."

"Ray?" I stepped toward the man, finally close enough to make out his features. It was Ray all right, still holding the rifle on his shoulder.

He slung the rifle back and gestured. "We gotta go."

I followed him up the slight embankment to reach Route 7. Surprised by the man's agility, I was winded but my body had finally warmed up after so much time in the river. "Wait," I said, "my friend is still in there."

"He's dead. Now let's move, unless you wanna join him."

I followed him across the road at a steady jog, ignoring the dim red-and-blue lights that strobed in my peripheral vision. I didn't want to believe it, but in my heart, I knew Ray was right.

We reached a driveway that I would have passed if Ray hadn't turned in. It was almost completely obscured by trees and bushes on both sides, more a narrow dirt path than a driveway. Another thirty yards and we came to a small but well-kept house crouching among the surrounding pines.

"Did you kill it?" I asked.

Ray turned, and in the harsh light thrown by the flood lamps mounted on the house, I saw stark terror on his face. "Don't know if it *can* be killed, but I hit it for sure."

"W-What *is* it?" I needed to know.

He shook his head but didn't answer.

The funerals were wretched affairs. Both sets of parents were coping badly with the loss of their sons, and the families shot looks at me that made me very uncomfortable. *Why did you get to live? Why didn't you save my son?* After a while, I kept my eyes downcast, even when speaking to them.

Ray had called the State Police to report the incident, saying he'd been getting home from work at the gas station when he'd spotted me staggering out of the woods. I told the police about the detour and the flat tires, leaving out any mention of the tack strip or the run-in with the local cop. The rest of my story was that the three of us had started walking toward the road when a bear charged out of the woods. We'd gotten separated and I was the only one to make it back to the road.

A search party had gone in but hadn't found any sign of Pat or Mark that night. The car was found, and there were questions about the broken headlights, and, of course, the beer, but I told a vaguely believable story about going off the road into a tree at some point. It was enough to satisfy the police. There was no tack strip mentioned in any reports. I assumed it had been removed the night before.

The following day, two bodies, both badly mutilated, were brought out of the woods. Looked like an animal attack, the staties said, and Officer Collier of the local PD, a veteran outdoorsman, agreed. "Definitely a bear attack," Collier was quoted as saying, "very uncommon, but not unheard of in these parts."

The day after the funerals, I got in my car—a 1973 AMC Hornet Coupe—and headed north. The solo trip to Bennington was a lonely one, split between survivor's guilt and a gnawing heartache for my lost friends.

I had been speaking with Ray almost daily since the incident. He had filled me in about his suspicion of Collier's involvement in providing victims for whatever it was that lived in those woods.

Ray had been holed up in a motel just across the Massachusetts border. His boss at the gas station said Collier had been in almost daily asking for him, becoming more insistent with each passing day. Ray and I met at the motel, drank coffee, and picked at take-out food until late afternoon. Then we loaded Ray's pick-up—including a very heavy duffel bag—and drove to his house. I would pick up my car after. If there *was* an after.

We stopped at the gas station where Ray worked, ostensibly for food and beer but mainly to be seen. Ray chatted it up with the guy working the pumps while I played Pac-Man. We were at Ray's house well before dark. Then, the waiting began. We hung out in the backyard, playing the radio loud and being deliberately visible. If anyone was watching the house for Collier—and Ray was sure they were—we would have visitors after dark.

Darkness fell quickly in the woods. One minute, bright shafts of sunlight were piercing the trees, the next, a heavy cloak fell and the sounds of the night erupted. Then, full dark. We went about working quickly and silently, going inside when the bugs became too aggressive no matter how much *Off!* we slathered on. Ray flipped on the outside floodlights and all the interior lights as well. It was showtime.

The waiting was brutal. Ray made a pot of coffee on the propane stove, bitching the whole time about needing to update the cabin before he blew the place up. Then he built up a nice fire in the wood stove; even though it was still August, nights could get pretty cold. We passed an hour playing cards at the kitchen table; the sense of being watched was like a physical presence in the room with us. The urge to turn around toward the direction of the windows was an itch I wanted to scratch. Finally, we turned off most of the lights and switched on the television, tuning in to the Red Sox game. So far, everything was going as planned. We hadn't expected anything to happen too early in the evening, there was too much traffic on Route 7, too much potential for witnesses.

All was silent outside for an hour-and-a-half, I figured, based on how much of the ball game had been played. I hadn't been paying attention to the game, only using it as a way to measure the time passing.

Mostly, I replayed the memory of handing Bennie the autographed Hulk picture. He'd stared at it, his hands shaking, tears slipping down his cheeks. Then he'd launched himself into my arms, sobbing. "Thank you," he'd said, over and over. Then the crying subsided into more of a quiet weeping. "Why me, Dave?" I had no answer.

A branch snapped outside. It could have been an animal, but I knew in my gut it wasn't. At least, not any run-of-the-mill Vermont woods animal. I glanced at Ray but he remained still, eyes forward. If he'd heard the sound, he made no indication.

A scraping sound came next, this from the back of the house—the branch snapping had come from the side. I smiled. *This might work out after all,* I thought. Then something else, footsteps on gravel, from the front of the house. There was more than one of them, or, maybe just the one and the cop. From my peripheral vision I saw that Ray remained stoic, focused. A nightbird called from outside, then all hell broke loose.

The front door exploded inward at the same time a loud SNAP! sounded from the back of the house, followed immediately by an inhuman howl of pain and rage. A figure moved quickly—too quickly to be human—toward the couch. Ray fired once from his spot in the loft and the creature's head disappeared in a splash of skull fragments, gray matter, and a gush of blood.

Two more of the creatures ran into the room. Ray hit one in

the shoulder with his shot but I never having shot a gun in my life—missed badly. The television exploded in a fireworks display of orange sparks, leaving the room in total darkness. I resisted the urge to keep firing, knowing I'd need the shots. We didn't know how many of the things were out there.

Ray army-crawled across the loft so he was looking down the flight of steps in case any of the creatures tried to attack. I remained motionless, waiting for my eyes to adjust to the darkness. The plan had worked perfectly. Under the cover of darkness, we'd propped up a decoy made from pillows and blankets to look like a pair of figures watching TV, then slipped up to the loft. Before that, Ray had set an old-fashioned bear trap outside the back door. He wasn't sure if it even worked, but the wail that had come on the heels of the trap springing told me it did. By my count, there was one creature dead, one wounded, and one in the trap, leaving at least one unhurt somewhere in the darkness below. We had guns and plenty of ammunition, provided there weren't a dozen or more of the creatures. *More waiting,* I thought, remaining vigilant as I began to be able to distinguish shapes in the room below.

Something moved, and I fired. The creature screamed, a chilling cry of pain that sounded human, then fell with a crash. I stifled a shout of triumph. Then came the realization that I'd just taken another's life. Granted, not human . . . but maybe only a step or two away in terms of evolution. I gagged, choking back hot bile but unable to stop the unexpected tears that came.

Ray whistled and signaled that he was going downstairs. He reached the bottom step with me right behind when a roar erupted from the front hallway. The creature leaped but Ray was faster. He'd seen it coming and had the rifle poised. The shot changed the creature's trajectory, sending it flying toward the living room, where it landed with a wet thump. That left only one that we knew of.

The back door was still closed and there hadn't been a sound from that direction since the shooting had started. Ray moved toward the door while I circled around in case there were others waiting to attack. I nodded when I was in position and Ray swung the door open. The shot was deafening and Ray was flung backward, a hole appearing in his back. I went down on one knee and started firing. Something groaned from just outside the door. I crept toward the back door. Once glance at Ray told me I didn't need to check on him, he'd been blown almost in half by the shot.

I reached the back wall next to the door. From that angle I could see a bloody hand and a cannon-sized pistol next to it. I took another step and the cop's head came into view. He wasn't dead, the shot had taken him in the meaty part of the chest below the collar bone. He was trying to reach the gun with his other hand but twisting his body was clearly causing him too much pain. He looked up, his grimace turning to rage. "You're dead, kid."

I barked out a surprised laugh, kicking the cop's gun well out of reach. I must have been in shock or experiencing some kind of adrenaline high, because my fear was gone. "Big talk from a guy with one leg in a bear trap and a bullet in his chest." I took a quick look behind me, still concerned about being ambushed by another creature, but there was no movement.

"There's more of them," the cop said, a mad grin on his face, "lots more. And they're coming. No fudgelling around."

"Then I guess I better get out of here," I said. Keeping my eyes on the cop, I backed up to the end table and grabbed Ray's keys. I'd take the truck back to the motel, switch it for my car, and be gone.

"I'll find you myself, you fucking candy-ass piece of Massachusetts shit. Hubbard Street in Malden, Massachusetts, to be exact."

An icy ball of dread formed in my gut, slippery and unpleasant. I gaped at the grinning cop. *I should have known.* Mark and Pat's names had been in the papers and the police reports. With the police department's resources at his disposal, of course he knew where I lived.

"I won't kill you, though, not right away. I'll start with your parents, then your little brother—"

He shut up when I pointed the gun at his head.

"You don't have the balls."

I looked around the cabin. We'd come so close . . . *How is any of this to be explained?* "It can't," I muttered. I knew what I had to do. I stoked the embers in the wood stove and threw in more logs, leaving the door to the stove open. Soon the blaze was back to a roaring fire.

"Hey," the cop said, "what the fuck are you doing?"

He continued yelling at me, rattling the chain that held the bear trap staked to the ground while I made sure all the windows were closed.

The cop was watching me, eyes wild, thrashing madly despite his injuries. I smiled and walked over to the propane stove in the kitchen. Using a large knife from the block on the counter, I cut the feeder hose to the stove. The gas leaked into the cabin with a deadly hiss, the odor instantly apparent.

"You little piece of shit, you can't leave me here!" The cop began tugging on the leg caught in the trap, ignoring the pain of the steel teeth as well as his gunshot wound.

"Whatcha Gonna Do When Hulkamania Runs Wild On You?" I said, then walked out the front door, closing it firmly behind me, the cop's screams and curses echoing in my ears. I started Ray's truck and pulled out onto Route 7. I flipped on the radio, finding John Parr's hit from the previous year, "St. Elmo's Fire," and cranked up the volume. "I'm coming home, Bennie," I whispered. A moment later, the sky behind me exploded in a ball of blue-orange flames.

GROUNDHOG SLAY

NICK KOLAKOWSKI

CHAPTER 1

THE FULL MOON, viewed from the bottom of the lake, is a shimmering silver blotch, impossibly distant. I dig my boots into the soft mud, bend my knees, and push off, rocketing toward that ghostly spotlight, startling fish in my path. Right before I break the surface, I throw my arms out to slow down, and the top of my head emerges with barely a ripple.

The night is quiet. Warm wind rustles the trees, accompanied by the deep croak of horny frogs seeking dates. I float, kicking my arms and legs as I dig deep in my damaged mind for anything that feels like contentment or—dare I say it—joy. A long time ago (too long), a guru with a long gray beard who smelled like weed and patchouli oil told me life's only mission was to find the calm center within yourself. It's the only nirvana that exists, he added.

Right after he gave me that pearl of wisdom, I slammed a blade through his skull, so if he had more wisdom to impart, I never heard it. I've never seen him again, either, which is odd and more than a little dispiriting. I'd rather have another conversation with him than kill the same camp counselors for the millionth time. I have big questions about why I'm here.

This time around, I'd probably spare the old man's life.

The moon traverses a few degrees along its orbit, and I still feel nothing even remotely resembling inner peace. With a sigh, I decide it's time to start the evening's activities. Rolling onto my stomach, I paddle for the point along the shore where I know the dock awaits. As usual, I am dressed in mechanic's coveralls, a pair of heavy boots, and old leather gloves, but none of it weighs me down overmuch, given my strength, and I only need a few minutes to reach my destination.

I know I'm close when I hear water slapping against the dock's rotting pilings. In another summer or two, the dock will probably collapse. If the universe smiles upon Lake Legionnaire that day, an empty-headed teenager will be standing atop that deathtrap, and they'll plunge to a quick and relatively painless end underwater. These kids, they have no idea what's in store for them: disease, heartbreak, perpetually empty bank accounts—along with the dread that sets up shop in your heart once you reach adulthood. When you get your first sense of what eternity really means. It's pure ignorance that makes them so infuriatingly happy.

I pause, treading water, one hand on a piling. I know they're up there, although I can't hear them yet. Just like I know the machete is waiting at the end of the dock, atop a tangle of rope, like an obedient pet.

A low whine: "Oh, come on, Trevor . . . "

"You come on, Suzie. What are you, chicken?" Trevor follows up this timeless witticism by clucking rapidly.

Suzie burbles, "Don't make fun of *me*."

Next up: some innuendos about Trevor's muscles and Suzie's bathing suit, followed by complaints about the campers, before they settle into the real business. I can't listen to this sad pantomime again. Gripping the piling, I hoist myself onto the dock.

Suzie and Trevor are dim shapes to my right, tangled together atop the whitish square of a towel. I retrieve the machete, testing its balance. The blade is rusty, but its edge is nice and sharp (it's always nice and sharp). I lurch forward, swinging the weapon for dramatic effect, and despite the ancient boards squealing beneath my feet, I'm almost on top of them before they notice.

"Oh shit!" Suzie screeches, scooting backwards on her elbows.

Trevor springs to his feet, fists raised, as if he has a chance against something like me. I raise the machete. Trevor grunts and backpedals, then turns and sprints into the night, his sandals slapping the dirt.

"Trevor!" Suzie screams. "Don't leave me behind you *diiiiiick*!"

I lower the machete.

Suzie scrambles upright, her arms crossed over her chest, wheezing with fear.

Leaning toward her, almost nose-to-nose, I rasp, "Boo."

With an eardrum-blasting shriek, she spins, drops to one knee, recovers, and sprints after Trevor. I wait, counting in my head. When I reach five, the woods echo with the dull thwack of a skull colliding with a tree trunk, followed by Suzie's startled howl of pain.

I glance at the moon. It has nothing to say, as usual. Striding off the dock into the woods, I veer to the left, toward the distant lights of the camp. The monster's coming, kids. The monster just can't stop.

CHAPTER 2

IF ALL THE other hundreds of versions of this night were any indication, it will take Trevor and Suzie anywhere from fifteen to twenty minutes to reach the camp and alert the others. The first building along my route is the Fun and Games Cabin, where generations of campers have gathered to play checkers and listen to records. With all the little tykes in their bunks, the counselors use the space to chill out.

Through the dusty windows, I see the old television on the bookshelf alongside the stacks of games, its dial turned to a news channel. The U.S. President is readying to give a press conference. I open my mouth, ready to mimic the leathery cowboy actor who the masses saw fit to elect Leader of the Free World (" . . . we set out to reverse the decline in morale in our armed forces, and we're doing it . . . "), but the figure who emerges from the screen's static snowstorm is different, soft-cheeked and boyish, the head topped with a newscaster's head of hair. Bending to the microphone, he syrups out banalities in a thick Southern accent ("I feel your pain . . . pain . . . pain . . . "), and my heart leaps.

I've never seen this Dixie-fried chump of a President before.

A different President—well, that's as big a shift as emerging from the lake to find two moons overhead.

Three teenagers slouch on the couch in front of the television. Another two lurk at a table in the rear. Thanks to the cabin's lack of air conditioning, they're all soaked with sweat, their hair stringy, their knees and hands crusted with the day's dirt. If the half-empty soda bottles and snack bags scattered around the room are any indication, their bloodstreams sing with caffeine, sugar, and cheap carbohydrates, which means they will run faster, which would drag this evening out if I wanted to kill them.

On the couch's middle cushion, a blonde boy juggles a game

controller. "Come on," he says, "I don't wanna watch Bubba talk about how he's knocked up another piece of trailer trash."

"That's disrespectful," snaps the redhead sitting next to him. "That man's the President, okay? And he actually seems to care."

"None of them cares about anything but power," grumbles a bespectacled kid sitting at a table behind them. "Read Howard Zinn, you don't believe me."

"Howard who?" asks the redhead.

"Screw it." The blonde boy leaps off the couch, bends to the stack of hardware beneath the television, and smacks a button on a video-game console. I notice another big difference: the console is shiny-white and much sleeker than the clunky black box that's always sat there before. The screen flickers, President Bubba replaced by a cartoon landscape, a little man in a red cap riding atop a green dinosaur.

It's a different year.

Same kids, same lake, but different year.

How is that possible? Trying to think of reasons makes my brain feel like an egg frying in a cast-iron skillet, crisping at the edges. I clutch my head, digging my fingers into my scalp, as a low moan slips between my gritted teeth. On the screen, the man in the little red cap dies, returns, dies, returns, dies again.

High-pitched screams from the woods to my right. Trevor and Suzie have fabulous lungs, and the kids in the cabin will hear them in a minute or two. I make my way past the cabins full of sleeping campers, not bothering to stick to the shadows. There's a gun locked in a safe in the main office, Crazy Jim Pembery's .45 automatic with an extra clip of hollow-point bullets, but there's only one key, it's clipped to Jim's belt, and Jim is glued to a barstool in town for another hour or two. If an enterprising counselor wants to attack me with a canoe paddle or a paring knife, they can go right ahead. I won't fight back. I'm trying for inner peace.

I arrive at the camp's front gate, its cheerful wooden sign lit by a single bare bulb. Masses of bugs swarm the light. I pause again, in a deeper darkness thrown by the stand of oaks to the left of the gate, listening and watching. Every so often, the local police await me here, their high-powered rifles ready to fill me with enough lead to turn me into a paperweight.

No cops in sight.

Things are looking up.

I have a destination in mind, and once I get there, I have no idea if what I'll find will allow me to break this hellish loop I'm trapped in, but I have no choice. I refuse to think maybe I deserve this hell after the acts I committed in the earliest rounds.

I stick to the woods as I parallel the dirt road that leads away from the camp. Two miles east, it links up with the paved road that connects to town. Crickets fall silent at my approach only to start again once I pass. Maybe this time will be different. Why not? There was a new President, after all. Who knows what else—

My boot lands on something round and metallic.

A faint click.

Well, this is a new one.

I've never encountered a land mine before, and I'm happy to report it hurts only a little as a thousand metal fragments slice apart your flesh and splatter it across the trees like a hundred-gallon bag of pasta sauce. In that millisecond before I become a juicy feast for all the animals stalking these woods, I wonder who could have known I'd walk this exact pathway.

Who's hunting me?

CHAPTER 3

I MADE A few mistakes in my first hundred resets. Killing all those campers. And all those townspeople. And all those cops. And the postman that one time. Also those military guys, in the few iterations where the National Guard dispatched a jeep to town. I did my best to spare our four-legged friends; although dogs dislike me, probably because I smell like lake mud and blood.

I lost count of how many lives I've ended around Lake Legionnaire during this infinitely repeating summer. Close to two hundred. Or maybe it's zero, because the next time I surface from the lake, everything is back to normal: Suzie and Trevor on the dock, the kids watching television and playing video games in the cabin, the townspeople trying to drink away the existential despondency that comes with living in a small town where the local steel mill shut down forty years ago.

During those first resets, I wasn't intelligent. You could say I barely possessed much of a brain at all, my thoughts burned away by a firestorm of rage, rage, rage about . . . well, I couldn't remember. I rose again and again from the lake, stalked the camp and town in a random pattern, killed anyone in my path, and died once some enterprising soul either crafted a remarkable trap or found a suitably heavy-gauge weapon.

A racoon has more tactical cunning than I did, sorry to say.

Then something amazing happened.

Before arriving at the amazing part, though, I had to die repeatedly. Say what you will about the youth, when you trap them in an isolated summer camp with an oversized maniac like yours truly, they quickly become masters of innovation. They'll lure you into a burning cabin or a swinging chainsaw trap, or trick you into stepping onto a chain that, once wrapped around your ankle, drags you into the depths of the lake. Once they shot me through the head with a spear gun, which at least was a faster demise than the Incredible Flying Chainsaw Trick. Whack!

Blackness. Then:

Lake bottom.

Shimmering moon.

Hunt, kill, die.

Blackness. Then:

Lake bottom.

Shimmering moon.

Hunt, kill, die.

Blackness. Then:

Lake bottom.

Shimmering moon.

Hunt, kill, die.

Again and again.

And then:

A night just like any other. Emerging from the lake, climbing onto the dock, I found Suzie and Trevor in their usual state of undress—and yet I lacked the requisite rage necessary to chop them into beer-infused sashimi. I could only stand and stare as they ran screaming into the night.

After they left, something like a voice compelled me to keep moving along the lakeshore. Midway around, on a rocky hill of elms, I found a cabin I'd never seen before. Barely larger than an outhouse, it lacked windows or signage.

I paused in front of it, hopelessly confused. Was this yet another trap?

I stood and waited. The frogs grumbled, the mosquitoes buzzed, but nobody breathed or coughed or shuffled in the underbrush. After an hour, I advanced and tried the door, which opened onto a dim interior lit only by a single shaft of moonlight stabbing through a small skylight overhead. The walls were lined with bookshelves, filled with hardcover volumes of every size and type:

Tolstoy.

Ellison.

Austen.

Orwell.

Golding.

Stevenson.

The entire classic canon, from Aristotle to Zola.

Not that I knew any of those names at the time, but I would learn. Who had built this amazing library in the middle of nowhere? Surely not any of the camp counselors. Although most of my interactions with them were brutal and short, they tended to do things like explore spooky basements alone, trip over their own feet at the worst moments, and climb into cars without checking the back seat for maniacs—all of which suggested they barely had the intelligence to read See Spot Run, much less assemble a treasure trove of knowledge.

My rage sank into a bottomless hole. I was a true Hollow Man, to quote Eliot. If I no longer wanted to slaughter people, what was I going to do now?

I plucked the closest book off the shelf, a dog-eared copy of Milton's "Paradise Lost" (annotated), and flipped to the first page, the first line: "Of Mans First Disobedience, and the Fruit . . . "

The dimness made it hard to read the tiny print, and I struggled with the words at first. How did I know how to read in the first place? No idea. I was two thousand lines into Milton's epic poem when the door burst open, framing two hunters in camouflage fatigues that barely managed to hold their beer bellies in check. I knew them: Rider and Pittman, two local yahoos who liked to shoot deer off-season, drink gallons of alcohol, and leer at the more attractive camp counselors.

I had killed them both fifty times, if not more. They were deer poachers, stalking near a summer camp filled with kids, totally unconcerned if an errant shot happened to snap through two hundred yards of woods and hit a little kid in the neck, which, to my thinking, made them more than worthy of death.

In the normal course of events, I would have run into them deep in the woods, where I always had the element of surprise on my side. The best way to surprise a redneck hunter is to kick his sister in the jaw. The second-best way is to drop from a tree behind him with a machete. But this time, they had the drop on me.

"The hell?" Pittman announced. "Kinda freak is that?"

I hadn't bothered to retrieve that machete from its usual space on the dock. I had no weapons, and no way to rise from a sitting position before they leveled their .30-06 rifles at me.

"Plug 'em good," Rider said, pulling the trigger.

Boom.

So much for relaxation.

Eyes open.

Lake bottom.

Shimmering moon.

When I restarted, I made my way back to the cabin and resumed Milton where I'd left off. Only this time, I placed the Merriam-Webster dictionary on the bench beside me—ten-plus pounds of English language. When Rider and Pittman slammed that door open, I was ready. Pittman barely had time to open his mouth before I dropped Milton, grabbed the dictionary, and slung it like the world's heaviest frisbee at his head. The book's spine connected with his front teeth, which cracked with an almost musical note.

Pittman stumbled back into Rider, their rifles askew. I was already on my feet, sprinting despite my enormous size, so fast that I caught the dictionary before it hit the ground, and, two-handed, brought it in a tight arc that ended with the back of Pittman's skull. With a loud pop of bone, he tumbled to the floor. Rider stumbled backward, tripped over the cabin's threshold, and fell onto the ground outside, his .30-06 skittering away.

I snatched up the weapon. A flicker of my old rage was returning, enough for me to think of something truly innovative. Rider shrieked as the barrel tore through the seat of his pants on its way up his tradesman's entrance. I'd like to think Milton would have approved of that finishing move, given his infernal imagination.

After double-checking that Pittman was also dead, I returned to my books for another five hours until a trio of freaked-out cops, probably alerted by Suzie and Trevor's stories of a homicidal creature lurking in the woods, blew the cabin (and me) apart with a couple of grenades.

Eyes open.

Lake bottom.

Shimmering moon.

The next fifty times, I swiped handfuls of books from the cabin before retreating into the woods to read. I could usually squeeze in four or five hours of reading by moonlight—sometimes until the break of dawn—before hunters or police or intrepid camp counselors found me. I was no longer quite so enraged. It was all hilarious, so hilarious I laughed every time they shot, stabbed, or set me on fire.

CHAPTER 4

THE FULL MOON SHIMMERS. I kick against the bottom, rising, thinking: who plants a land mine near a summer camp? Didn't they know a kid could step on it? Imagine trying to explain to a pair of distraught parents that Little Jimmy took a wrong step and can now fit into a tiny plastic bag.

The land mine was for me, of course. But how could they have known I'd walk that way? I shift constantly, drifting wherever the muse takes me, while everyone else follows their preset patterns.

Except maybe that's wrong.

Maybe there's someone out there just like me, watching, waiting, aware of the loops and my every move . . .

I swim across the lake, climb the dock. Suzie and Trevor scream and run. I trot to the cabin window so I can double-check on the President—yep, still the good ol' boy with the great hair—before I head through the camp to the road. At the camp's gate, I'm seized by a paranoia so intense it's paralyzing. How do I know my mysterious pursuer hasn't seeded land mines in different spots?

Well, vaporization by shrapnel stings a lot less than a psychic kid slowly tearing you apart with her telekinetic abilities. Remember that hilarious encounter? You can handle anything, you big baby.

I step into the middle of the dirt road. Insects hum, frogs grunt. No explosion. Good. Time for the next part of my master plan: make it to town, find a vehicle, and drive to the far side of the lake, where the solution to my eternal torment might await. I try not to think about how I've never survived much past dawn.

I march, not bothering to stick to the shadows, hoping that whoever planted that land mine wasn't enough of a psychotic lunatic to scatter a few in random spots. Two miles later, my feet hit pavement.

I know from previous experience it'll take an hour along this two-lane to reach town. There's only the moon shining off the road's yellow line, which I follow, figuring a driver will stop if they see me. You'd be surprised at the folks who will step on the brakes for a hulking brute with a face that looks like it did twelve rounds with an electric fan. Never underestimate a long-haul trucker's need for a little companionship, if you know what I mean.

But no trucker arrives. Instead, I'm greeted by a tall figure astride the center line, his face shadowed by a ten-gallon cowboy hat, his thumbs hooked into his belt loops, his cowboy shirt crisscrossed by two bandoliers of ammunition. His rhinestone high-heeled boots glitter in the moonlight. When he sees me, he strides forward, unslinging an AR-15 rifle from behind his back.

"Well, it's you," he calls out.

I am in zero mood for a High Moon standoff in the middle of Rural Route 1. But when I open my mouth to tell him to move, a glut of stinking lake water explodes up my throat. Instead of warning this clown off, I spend the next few seconds coughing and drooling like an idiot. My lungs finally clear, I try again: "Who the hell are you?"

The cowboy stops, his head jerking back, as if punched. "You talk?"

"You plant that land mine?" I ask, marching forward. "You know some kid could have stepped on that, you idiot?"

"You talk?"

I am clearly not dealing with a genius intellect here.

"Long is the way and hard, that out of Hell leads up to light," I offer.

He squints. "You sound like a garbage disposal."

Blame that on my throat, thick with scar tissue and probably some plant matter from the bottom of the lake. "What is dark within me, illumine," I roar, spewing saliva everywhere.

"Don't assault my ears with that Shakespeare shit." The man raises his rifle. "And I don't know nothin' about no land mine."

After so many hundreds of times repeating the same scenarios (lake, splash, hack, die), I feel an odd elation at all this newness around me. It's too bad the newness seems intent on blasting me apart at every opportunity.

"Name's Joe Bubba Leonard," the man announces, his finger sliding around the trigger. "You mighta hearda me, you hellish abomination. I run the best drive-through in all of Texas, I'm hell with any gun, and I devoted whatever life I got to endin' evil freaks like you."

"You must be kidding," I say.

Joe Bubba Leonard tilts his head back to study me, revealing a jaw as square as a bulldozer shovel and shiny sideburns worthy of Elvis. The moonlight reflects off a silver pin clipped to his shirt pocket: a slouching figure with long arms dangling past the knees, like a stretched-out ape.

"Seriously," I add. "I don't have time for this crap. Move, okay?"

Instead of answering, Joe Bubba Leonard points the rifle at me and pulls the trigger.

Bang.

The bullet carves a chunk of meat from my left shoulder.

I stride forward, undeterred despite my left arm flopping loose, the tendons shredded. I might not want to kill anyone tonight, but I'll buy this idiot a one-way ticket to Cripple Town if he keeps firing at me.

Joe Bubba Leonard's perfect jaw flops open, and he shakes his smoking rifle. "But . . . but . . . that was a silver bullet."

"Do I look like a motherfucking werewolf?" I say, closing in.

"Damn it," he says, and fires again. This shot glances off my thigh, scraping some bone along with skin and cloth and flesh. Despite his boasting, he's terrible at aiming. The wound hurts enough to make me wince a little, but I'll heal quickly. It's part of the whole revenant thing.

"The definition of insanity," I say, "is doing the same thing over and over again, expecting different results."

"Christ on a cracker." Joe Bubba Leonard retreats. "You're the first one I met that talks."

I almost stop in my tracks. "First one?"

"I shot Cripple the Bigfoot!" He yells. "His pelt hangs on the wall of my box office, and it ain't no bearskin like everybody says! I killed Big Jim—that giant eel-lookin' bastard up in Okanagan. None of 'em talk. What makes you different?"

"I can read," I tell him, which is true. I'm almost close enough to grab him before he can fire again.

Recognizing the danger, Joe Bubba Leonard backs up, the rifle barrel wavering in my direction but his finger drifting off the trigger. His eyes glaze as his brain spits back an error message. I remember reading *Dracula* twice, captivated by the descriptions of Van Helsing, the elegant monster hunter, erudite at the dining table yet savage in the crypt. The quality of monster hunters has tumbled in the past century, or maybe I just have the misfortune of facing down the wrong one.

We've reached the road's curve when a deeper rumbling begins, barely louder than the idiot song of insects. Transfixed by my approach (I have that effect on people), Joe Bubba Leonard starts yelling again, naming more creatures he's supposedly reduced to skins on the walls of his drive-in's office. I'm tempted to tell him about the noise, to wake up, but I suspect I'll see him again soon, no matter what happens.

" . . . and then I killed me a Jersey Devil right after introducing a Peckinpah double feature in South Jersey, and I tried a .357 Magnum but it didn't work so I had to bust my dynamite nut," a smirk flashes across his face. "I got a whole arsenal, so don't come closer or I swear . . . "

As the road brightens and the roar intensifies enough to drive the insects to silence, I decide to say something, because while I might be a mass-murdering monster from beyond time and space,

I'm not a total sadist. Unfortunately, just a single word manages to escape my lips in that last quarter-second: "Watch—"

Joe Bubba Leonard, hero of the late-night B-movie marathon and terrible shot with an AR-15, only manages to turn his head an inch before a hurricane of light veers around the curve.

I've been hit by trucks at least twice. It hurts surprisingly less than you might think, mostly because an 18-wheeler moving at seventy miles an hour will pulverize you before your nerves can send any pain signals to your brain. Joe Bubba Leonard barely squawks as the enormous fender plows into him, knocking him clean out of his fancy rhinestone boots.

I step aside as the truck booms past, close enough for me to kiss the trailer. The trucker never slows down, never honks his horn. I understand. When you're hauling ass between Los Angeles and Boston, your blood singing with enough quality speed to keep a battalion of Marines awake for a week, you might have a hard time determining what's a trick of the drugs and the night. A tall man in a cowboy hat and shiny boots, toting a rifle, who appears out of the dark just long enough to disappear beneath your fender? Best not to wonder if it was a figment of your subconscious (Hi Daddy!) as you zoom onwards toward dawn.

Once the truck disappears around the next curve, I examine the road. The rhinestone boots still stand on the center line. The cowboy hat, its brim slightly crumpled, floats onto the gravel shoulder. Joe Bubba Leonard was a big guy but the boots likely won't fit my size-14 feet. The cowboy hat, though, slides over my scalp quite nicely.

I find what's left of Joe Bubba Leonard in a ditch. At least the truck's impact left his handsome features largely intact. I root in his moist pockets, pulling out a white leather wallet (slightly stained) with the words 'BAD HOMBRE' in tiny pink rhinestones on the front. Joe Bubba Leonard might have been a bad hombre, but he was also a broke one, because in addition to his driver's license and a coupon good for one (1) lap dance at someplace called Golden Chubby's, I find only seven dollars in bills. I have better luck with the other pocket, which yields a rabbit's foot keychain. One of the two-dozen keys dangling from it has a Ford logo on the fob.

Leaving the mess behind (dinner's on me, bugs and varmints), I hunt for Joe Bubba Leonard's vehicle, which I discover on a dirt access road maybe fifty yards beyond where he first confronted me.

It's a bright yellow truck, orange flame decals rippling along its sides, with monster tires and a rack of powerful lights behind the cab.

I unlock the driver's door and climb in. The interior features leopard-print seats, a pair of fuzzy dice dangling from the rearview mirror, and a werewolf decal on the purple dashboard. Every inch of it is a crime against good taste, but I don't care so long as it drives.

The engine roars to life at the first twist of the key, and I shift into first gear and ease onto the main road. I have no idea where I learned to drive a stick shift. Much about my past eludes me, lost in the chaos of loop after loop. Of course, there's also the biggest question of all: Why am I here? Because every monster has its origin story, no? The abusive family of inbred hicks in the backwoods, the mad scientist tooling around in the laboratory during a lightning storm, an accident with toxic waste and a piece of fungus—you'd think I'd remember at least a fragment. Yet as hard as I try to think back to the beginning, nothing ever comes.

The town appears so quickly it's almost shocking. In yet another sign I'm finally in a different year, what was formerly a sleepy strip of small stores, barely lit by yellow lights at either end of Main Street, now blazes with neon and halogen lighting. I rumble past a gas station and three fast-food places, still open despite their empty parking lots.

My stomach rumbles with hunger. This is an unusual feeling. Eating is rarely part of my usual routine. For all I know, my stomach is full of lake mud, spent ammunition, seaweed, and a camper's finger or two. But if I want my left arm to heal, I'll need calories. I pull into the first drive-thru along the way.

"Wha wan?" The speaker blurts.

I squint at the menu pinned behind the sun-yellowed plastic. "Burger."

A long sigh. "Wha kin burger?"

At second glance, the burger menu is rather long. I could order The Rattler (two "slabs" of bacon atop a twelve-ounce beef patty) or opt for the Double Whammy (two patties straining under the weight of a pile of onion rings). Everything is three bucks or less, which fits my budget.

"Rattler," I say.

"Drin?"

"Wha?"

"Wanna drin?"

"Wha?"

"Drin, man. Coke?"

Between my scarred vocal cords and the speaker's static, it's a two-way battle to understand anything. "No," I say.

"Twofitty," the speaker snaps. "Drive through."

I roll forward. Too late, I realize my impulsive quest for food might doom me. No matter how weird the customers who pull up to the drive-thru window on a typical night, I doubt any of them has a pretty face like mine. If things get weird, I could yank the employee through the little window and pull off their head like a bottlecap, but this truck's interior is too clean and dry to ruin in good conscience, and besides, I'm still aspiring to inner peace.

I arrive at the window. The pimply teenager behind the register hands me a greasy bag without bothering to so much as glance in my direction. I guess some real mutants lurk around these parts. Tossing over the cash, I drive away without waiting for my change, already tearing through the moist bag with my free hand.

I down the burger's heavenly meat in two huge bites as I pull back onto the road. With town and its glimmering lights in my rearview mirror, I enter a deeper darkness, bugs splattering the windshield like gummy rain.

The burger finished, I toss the wrapper into the passenger footwell. I slap my hand against the glove compartment until the lid flops open. Inside, nestled among the crumpled menus and receipts and driver's registration, rests an enormous silver pistol. Some "arsenal." I'm getting the idea that ol' Joe was overcompensating for something.

I don't like guns, and not just because I've been shot a couple hundred times. Say what you will about knives, chainsaws, and rocks, at least you need to get close to do the work. To get a little wet. That closeness means a certain respect for your prey, even if they're a screeching moron who thought they were safe behind a bathroom door barely thicker than a sheet of paper.

I slam the glovebox closed. When I look up again, the truck's cabin fills with bright white light—headlights behind me. I downshift and brake, angling for the shoulder so this speed demon can pass. Imagine my surprise when they ram into my rear fender hard enough to transform Joe Bubba Leonard's garish truck into a hillbilly rocket.

CHAPTER 5

ON ONE OF the more recent loops, I did something unusual.

I knew that, no matter what actions I took around the camp, eventually I would meet a grisly end at the hands of cops, hunters, or overcaffeinated campers. I'd read every book in the peculiar cabin, and one of the last titles had been Sartre's "No Exit." *L'enfer, c'est les autres*. Hell is other people. So why play the game?

I decided to swim for the far side of the lake. In the darkness, with a low fog drifting over the water, I quickly lost my way. Not that it mattered: My strength gave me the ability to paddle for untold hours, until black trees loomed against the starry sky. The faint lapping of water against rocks. I stopped kicking and my body drifted upright, my feet skimming the mud.

I walked ashore. Once I made it a few hundred yards into what seemed like endless woods, I tried to orient myself a bit more. I recalled an old map pinned to a bulletin board in the camp's HQ cabin: A federal preserve along the lake's northern rim, thousands of acres extending all the way to the state border. An equally huge expanse of logging territory sat alongside it. If this was where I'd ended up, nothing but logging roads and perhaps a park ranger's cabin awaited me for the next four hundred miles.

This presented something of a conundrum. I enjoyed the idea of walking forever without anyone trying to kill me. Maybe I could survive past dawn for once. But the prospect of endless walking was also boring as almighty hell—so boring that I halfway considered walking back to the lake and figuring out how to drown myself, just to reset everything again.

Even though I knew my deaths were temporary, the prospect of yet another burst of suffering, followed by the eyeblink of disorienting black, was enough to stop any thoughts of self-termination. If I was lucky, I might run into a bear large enough to swipe my head off with an enormous paw. That would be a first, at least. When you're trapped in a forever loop, you get your kicks where you can.

I crunched through the underbrush, not caring how much noise I made or what animal might await. The moonlight was strong enough to clearly outline every tree and bush. I crunched through a dense thicket of thorny vines—and stopped, startled.

Such an odd thing, being startled.

In front of me ran a chain link fence, maybe ten feet tall, its top lined with razor wire. Behind it stood tall poles at fifty-foot intervals. It all looked brand new, the metal shining, the chain link tight.

Rustling to my left. I swiveled in that direction. A deer's flank disappeared behind an oak. When I shifted my attention forward again, I noticed a small yellow plaque pinned to the fence.

It read: "Government Property. Keep Out. Lethal Force Authorized."

It didn't strike me as a sign the National Park Service would put up, unless those green-hatted little scamps had decided to transform into a special forces unit. Imagine a bunch of campers lighting an illegal fire so they can roast some marshmallows only for a Park Ranger to show up with a grenade launcher and an ultimatum.

No, this was federal land, and *los federales* were doing something very shady here. Worth exploring? I had nothing better to do tonight.

I climbed the fence, not caring how the razor wire slashed my flesh. Perhaps there was another kind of wire lining the top, or maybe they had installed sensors in the woods that detected the movement of anything larger than a squirrel. It's the only way to explain what happened in the next few moments.

On the far side of the fence, I faced a hillside thick with fallen logs, jagged rocks, and thorn bushes. Not impossible to climb, but certainly difficult. To my right, a narrow ravine cleaved the hill in two, seeming to offer easier passage to whatever lay beyond—although as I approached, I found it was likewise jammed with ancient trees. Nature had created a barrier far more effective than chain link and sharp metal.

I started walking again. As my prey will tell you, I am slow, sometimes plodding, but I get there. At the top of the hill, beyond a pyramid of ancient logs, the trees fell away before an overgrown field. Beyond the field, two more chain link fences ringed a complex of massive buildings, white and windowless.

Nope, definitely not Park Rangers.

I marched forward, planning on climbing the fences. Except the first fence had metal signs bolted to it at intervals, each with a lightning bolt symbol. Electrified. No doubt with enough voltage to grill me into a crispy bit of barbecue.

I needed a gate. The fence seemed to go on forever as I followed it around, and as I did, I had a better view of the complex. A long white tube of some sort—maybe three stories high—ran between the buildings. I'd never seen anything like it.

Fifty yards later, bright lights popped to life, so blinding I threw a hand in front of my eyes.

Deep in the woods, branches and leaves crunched. Voices yelling. It sounded like dozens of men, angry, shouting orders.

I knew what was coming next. With a sigh, I let my arms drop.

"Oh, come *on*—" is all I had time to say before a hurricane of bullets smashed through me. I toppled backwards, glimpsing bits of me sizzling on the fence, blue smoke drifting into the night sky. I smelled pretty good. Beyond my blackened meat, a line of fighters advanced from the woods—men not dressed in army camouflage or cop blue but black fatigues and body armor, their faces covered with gas masks.

CHAPTER 6

BACK IN THE current loop, I'm stunned to find myself still alive and in one piece, despite the crunchy demise of Joe Bubba Leonard's truck. I'm also upside-down, pinned in place by my locked seatbelt. For an ordinary human being, this would present a problem, but I'm gifted with enough strength to grip the buckle and tear it free of the housing. I tumble against the steering wheel.

A disconcerting smell of gas fills the car. Of all the ways I've died during these loops, burning to death is probably worst, with having your head telekinetically ripped off by a strange ten-year-old a very distant second. With that in mind, I move carefully, twisting my torso so I flow through the broken driver's window into the grassy ditch where the truck ended up.

What happened to the vehicle that plowed into me? It must have been large—how else could it have flipped Joe Bubba Leonard's rolling bachelor pad?

I lurch onto the road, my left knee popping with every step. To the north, the moonlight reflects off metal and glass at the road's far curve: a huge pickup truck, its lights and engine off. If this is the prick who rammed into me, why is he waiting around?

The familiar rage flickers deep in my gut, ready to bloom into a comforting fire. No, calm down. Inner peace, remember? Besides, your anger makes you stupid. It's the only reason those camp counselors and townspeople manage to splatter you pretty much every time. Whoever rammed you off the road, they might not want to kill you—otherwise they would have ended you in the truck.

I'm within a few yards of the pickup when its door opens and a woman steps out: short, dark, her shiny hair pulled back in a tight ponytail. She wears a black t-shirt and a new pair of jeans, along with heavy hiking boots. In her left hand, she holds a .45 automatic.

"Hello," she says. It's hard to see her face in the dimness, but she sounds calm, perhaps too calm when almost toe-to-toe with something like me.

I advance. Twenty feet away now, then fifteen.

"That's not in your best interest," she says, still calm.

Fifteen feet, ten.

She raises the pistol and says, "You want to break the loop?"

I stop.

"I know all about it." She smiles. "How many times you been through? Ten thousand? Twenty thousand?"

"I don't remember," I say. The crash must have impacted my throat in some way, shifted tissues into a new position, because my voice is surprisingly clear.

She takes a step back, her eyebrows raising. Startled. "You speak well."

"Had the best education," I say. "Like Frankenstein's monster, but the book, not the movies."

She stuffs the gun into the holster on her waistband. "I had no idea," she said. "I would've tried to reach you some other way."

"The land mine," I say. "That was you?"

"Yes. And now I'm sorry for doing it. Not to overuse a cliché, but it's been a bit of a learning process for me."

"You better talk," I say. "The night's not young anymore."

"Do you eat?" She asks. "You want a cup of coffee? Something more substantial?"

The truth is, I do, despite the burger. Hundreds of loops ago, when I was still figuring out the parameters of my world, I made the hilariously dumb mistake of walking into a few establishments, including a few bars and the local diner. Maybe I thought that because this is America, people would snicker and cringe at my appearance, but serve me once they saw my money was green. Instead, I was met with bartenders firing shotguns at me and even a waitress shouting something about the Lake Man returning.

"Maybe not the best idea," I say.

"Oh, I think it's a great idea," she retorts, nodding at her truck. "Climb on in. I know a place. It's one county over."

This could still be a trap—but if so, it's so elaborate that I'm curious more than cautious. As I climb into the passenger side, the truck's shocks wheeze under my weight. There's a black cardboard box on the dashboard. Sliding into the driver's seat, she says, "That's for you. I apologize in advance, but it's necessary."

I open the box, which is lined with black velvet. Resting inside, a white half-mask, covering the eyes and brow. "Very Phantom of the Opera," I say, slipping it on. The nylon string bites into the back of my scalp and the eyeholes are a little small, but it will do.

"Can't do anything about your clothes," she says. "The mask, though, it'll dissuade some folks from asking. If anyone asks, that is. Frankly, I'm betting this place will be almost empty."

"What's your name?" I ask.

"Natalie." She starts the truck.

"And what do you want?"

"I need you to help me save the world."

CHAPTER 7

WE DRIVE THROUGH the humming night, down empty country roads, not saying anything to one another. We snap past a sign announcing the county line, perking me up. This is the farthest I've gotten from the lake in quite some time, if ever.

We arrive at an intersection and Natalie takes a left. A mile later, we pull into a gravel parking lot in front of a restaurant: Big Porky's House of BBQ, its peaked roof topped with a pink neon pig. Its yellow walls stained by years of smoke and grime, its steam-milky windows lined with strings of multicolored holiday lights. A true dive, if there ever was one.

Instead of taking us through the front door, Natalie gestures for me to follow her around the side. I've slipped on the Phantom of the Opera mask, but who knows whether it'll placate anyone we encounter. A mask never changes who you are.

Strings of lights on tall poles mark the boundaries of the dining area behind Big Porky's. At picnic tables nearest the restaurant's back door, a cluster of men and women hunch over trays of ribs and chicken wings, noisily stripping meat from bone. They're too busy eating and talking to notice us as we take the farthest table.

Natalie plucks one of the laminated menus tucked between the paper napkin dispenser and the bottles of hot sauce. "If I were you, I'd go for the three-meat platter, rib tips, beef brisket, burnt ends. You're a big guy, you could use the protein, I'm guessing."

"I'm vegetarian."

"What?"

"I'm kidding." I take the menu from her, curious if she'll flinch when my scarred hand brushes hers, pleased when her face remains impassive. "That platter is fine."

"Okay, I'll get the food. Back in a minute."

Once she disappears inside, I hide my face behind the menu. I'm oddly afraid one of the folks out here will focus on me, kicking off a chain of events that will inevitably lead to messy death. It's funny something like that would concern me. Maybe sitting here in a restaurant like a normal person, studying a menu, is exerting a civilizing influence on me.

Natalie returns with two trays balanced precariously in her hands. "Got us some cornbread," she says, placing the trays down and taking a seat across from me. Each of her hip pockets has a beer can, and she sets those on the table. "I figured you drink."

"Sure."

"Excellent. Cheers." Popping the tab of her can, she takes a deep swig. "Okay, question time. You ready?"

"Okay." I nibble a burnt end, and it's incredible, so incredible that I regret not spending my loops eating more meat.

"What's your name?"

I shrug. "I don't remember."

"What about a childhood? Parents? Anything like that?"

I shrug again. "Nothing."

"How many times have you died and come back?"

"I don't know. Thousands, definitely."

"Huh." She takes a mouthful of cornbread, chews it, swallows. "Huh."

"I never live very long."

"You're killed?"

I nod. "Within hours. Always by someone different. Kids, townspeople, cops. The Army, once or twice." I debate whether to tell her about the weird complex on the other side of the lake, with its security personnel dressed in black, and think better of it. Maybe she's one of them.

"You think there was anything weird about that?"

"Yes. Even when I'm trying to be alone, they come after me." There's no way I'll tell her about killing hundreds of people. For starters, nothing makes a meal worse than someone at the table confessing to mass murder. Second, I suspect she knows everything I've done, somehow.

"And you've never questioned why?"

I shrug yet again, like I want to give my shoulder muscles a real workout. I'm feeling defensive, which is unusual for me. "Because I am what I am." Meaning: a monster.

"What if I told you that it's all deliberate?"

"Uh, yeah, it's deliberate. They were deliberately trying to kill me."

"No, I mean," she waves a bone around. "All of this, the world, it's actively trying to kill you. Pardon me for saying so, it's as if you're a virus, and everyone who ends up taking you out—the cops or the camp counselors or whoever—is the immune system."

I chew while I think about it. "Sure."

Her eyebrows pop up. "Sure?"

"It works as well as any theory. I've seen it all. I'm open to anything."

"Because the same thing's been happening to me." She glances at the folks at the next table. "I've managed to make it for a day and a half, at most, before something takes me out. A car wreck or someone with a gun. Doesn't matter."

"So, you're stuck in these loops."

"Yes. Twenty-one times and counting."

"I thought it was just me."

"It sounds like you've been stuck in here a lot longer than me."

"Yes." I sip my beer. "Yes, it does."

"And you've never questioned why any of this is happening to you?"

"No, I have . . . " I want to tell her about the guru with the long gray beard who told me about the emptiness of nirvana and never appeared again; about the cabin in the woods with its infinity of books; about the new President on the television in the cabin. But she might not understand any of it if she's only been through this horrific wash-rinse cycle a few times. "It just kept happening and happening, and so I just . . . gave up asking."

"It's like 'Groundhog Day,'" she says. "That movie with Bill Murray? It's so good."

"More like 'Groundhog Slay.'"

"Hey, you have great wordplay skills. Movies aside, there's something much larger going on. I mean, obviously." She sips her beer. "Once we're done eating, I want to show you something. Maybe you can make sense of it. I sure as hell can't. I just know it's dangerous as hell. Maybe world-ending dangerous."

"What did you do?" I ask. "I mean, before the loop. What was your job? Where are you from?"

"I'm from Boise, Idaho. I'm an FBI agent. I like red wine, cats, and sending bad guys to jail. I was on vacation up here when I died, then woke up again. Now it's just . . . repetition. Don't you hate it?"

"Yes." And yet, I can't remember anything different. No wonder I'm so full of rage.

"Then let's figure a way out." She smothers her meat with barbecue sauce, forks it onto a slice of white bread, and wolfs it down. I do the same. Can I trust this woman? Have I ever had a friend?

As I finish my meat, a question occurs to me: "Talk about the land mine."

"Yes." She holds up a hand, her fingers stained red with sauce. "Again, I'm sorry about it. Have you ever encountered a man named Joe Bubba Leonard? Kind of a weird character, dresses and talks really big?"

I nod.

"He gave it to me when I flashed my badge. He's got a whole arsenal of that stuff. Calls himself a cryptozoologist, of all things. I thought you'd step on it, realize you were on a land mine, and not move until I got there. Then we could have a conversation. But his land mine, maybe it was handmade or wired wrong or something like that, because it blew—you blew—pretty much immediately."

"It's okay," I say.

"Really? Because I feel really bad about it, like I said. The biggest piece I found of you was a thumbnail. I shot myself in the head, right there. Figured I'd reset quicker that way. Next time around, I rushed to meet Joe Bubba Leonard, mostly because I wanted to kick some sense into him. I saw him get splashed all across that road. Then I chased you down."

"You knew I wouldn't kill you?"

Now it's her turn to shrug. "I figured you might. But hey, I'd just come back again, right? What I've learned from my years in the FBI is that if you're in a tense situation with someone, you always give them a way out that doesn't involve violence. Chances are good they'll take it. I'll take your tray."

She stands, stacking my empty tray on hers. At the other table, one of the women turns to look at us and does a cartoonish double take. She bends to whisper in the ear of the man next to her, who does his best to side-eye us without making it seem obvious. I recall what Natalie said about immune systems, how this world wants to wipe me out at every opportunity. If that's the case, perhaps all my killing is in self-defense. Maybe I should kill everyone at that table right now—

Warmth on my wrist: Natalie touching me, her brow furrowed with concern. "No," she says. "Let's just leave."

"Okay." I nod. I'll try it her way. What do I have to lose?

"Meet me by the car," she says. "I got to use the bathroom before we go." Picking up our trays and cans, she heads for the back door.

I fade into the darkness beyond the picnic tables. The urge to flee into the woods, to abandon Natalie and this weird quest, is almost overpowering. Only I know the clock will tick down to zero and fate will send a truck or bullet or improvised spear in my direction. At least with Natalie, I'm not alone.

By the time I reach Natalie's truck, I also feel, for the first time in a thousand loops or more, a tingle of excitement. What if I find some answers? Or even a personal nirvana of some kind? Absolutely worth it.

The front door of Big Porky's thumps open, framing Natalie in a rectangle of yellow light. She looks angelic. Bouncing her keys from hand to hand, she stops in front of me. "Ready?"

"As I'll ever be."

She unlocks the door. "We'll see about that. We'll just see."

CHAPTER 8

NATALIE PEELS OUT of the parking lot in a squeal of burnt rubber and a spray of gravel, spinning so hard into the turn it feels like the truck might tip over. Bumping into the proper lane, she stands on the gas, accelerating us to eighty miles an hour—too fast for these narrow country roads. As much as I like to think that nothing can frighten me, she really tests the limits of my calm as she steers into curve after curve, tires rumbling on the shoulder, practically daring the universe to throw a deer or hitchhiker in our way.

"The third time I looped around," she says. "I tried to commit suicide. Well, not really. It was more of an experiment, if anything. I stole a Porsche—yes, I was able to find a Porsche, even in an armpit town like this, if you can believe it—and I got it up to a hundred thirty on the highway before a tire blew on me. I went right into a guardrail, ripped the car open like a tin can." She laughs. "It was hilarious."

"Yeah, sounds like a laugh riot."

"By that point, I knew I was coming back. I just wanted to work out my frustrations."

"Slow down, please."

"Aw, you're no fun." She taps on the brakes until the truck settles down to a more reasonable fifty, the woods no longer a blur. Without the euphoria of speed, her smile fades, her gaze cooling. "Can I ask you a serious question?"

"Yes."

"Promise you won't be angry."

"I will do my best."

"Why'd you kill all those people?"

I'm startled. "How do you know about that?"

"How can I not know about that? You're a local legend. Joe Bubba Leonard couldn't stop talking about you. Said you'd be a bigger catch than Bigfoot."

"But . . . " I'm flummoxed, if that's the right word. Another emotion I haven't felt in a long, long time.

"But what?"

"This loop . . . it's just tonight. It's all I've ever known."

"You don't remember anything before, right?"

"Right."

"Well, you must have done something before you got stuck in the loop, because Joe Bubba Leonard said you'd been stalking the lake for years, killing campers and anyone else who got in your way. You've had all sorts of names. The Lake Man. The Chopper. He even made up some Native American names for you, but that's a bunch of crap . . . right?"

"I don't know." Maybe I've existed for centuries, but how is that possible? Nothing lives that long.

"Okay." She frowns—disappointed? Angry at me? "But you've killed people tonight, right?"

"Yes." I bow my head.

"Why is that?"

"Because I was angry. Confused. All those things." I scramble to fill her stony silence. "For what it's worth, I knew with the loop that they'd just come back again. They were haunting me, in a way. I could kill them, but then they'd just come back. I couldn't escape them."

She shakes her head. "I don't know, it's still pretty messed up."

"And yet you're here."

"And yet I'm here. But you need to make me a promise, okay?"

"What?"

"No more killing. Not unless it's necessary. Heck, not even then. You'll just come back."

"They come back."

"Good point. Just . . . let's just try not to cause too much chaos, okay? We might seem like we're endlessly repeating; but we might be having impacts we can't recognize. Butterfly effect and all that."

"Butterfly what?"

"You've never heard of that? Butterfly flaps its wings in Tokyo, causing a hurricane in the Dominican Republic? Small effects ripple and ripple until they're wrecking the world?"

"I'm just the Lake Man, remember?"

"Well, think on it. We're here." Bumping the truck onto the shoulder, she kills the engine. We've stopped beside a patch of woods thick with pines and thorn bushes. No electric lights or other signs of civilization. She climbs out, tapping her pistol grip as she does so—a nervous tic. I follow her, pausing after I shut the door so I can take full measure of the night. The whispering of pine branches on rocks, the moon spilling its silvery light over the slope beyond the brush.

If I stand still for hours, my concentration deepens to a cellular level, until I can hear the worms and grubs shoveling their tunnels through the blackness beneath the leaves. I can sense a frightened boy's heart thrashing against his ribs as if it were my own. Given enough time, I can even smell the syrupy xylem and phloem seeping up within each tree trunk. Sensations so intense you lose yourself in them—and I have, at least until some redneck interrupts me with a load of buckshot.

Natalie pauses before a gap in the pines. "I think this is the way," she says, squinting. "Yeah, that's it. Come on."

She picks her way down a narrow path, careful to avoid the sharper stones and treacherous flows of gravel. I crash through the underbrush on a diagonal, the smaller branches smacking against my Phantom of the Opera mask, thorns spiking deep into my flesh. I meet her as she reaches the bottom of the slope, where the trees open into a wide clearing.

The clearing's edges are ragged and the trees along its perimeter are bent, as if something massive impacted in the middle of it, but there's no sign of a crater or fire. I take a cautious step beyond the trees, noting how all the branches bend in the same direction—along with the weeds and bushes at my feet. Every plant tilted at an angle of forty-five degrees toward the clearing's center.

The wind picks up, rustling against my back. Except there's something odd about it. Not the soft rustle and moan of air on the move. No, it's more of a whistling. Like what you hear from a cave entrance. Only it seems to come from above us.

"Look at this," Natalie says, bending to scoop a handful of soil. She stands and opens her fingers, but the dirt doesn't trickle to the ground. Instead, it rises from her palm, spinning into a miniature tornado that snaps away into the dark.

"I don't get it."

"Look up. Right overhead. You'll see."

I follow her orders. In the deep woods, with no light pollution, the sky glitters with stars—except for an inky-black splotch partially obliterating the Big Dipper. I step to my left, and the constellation's missing stars reappear. I squint and say, "It's like there's a hole in the sky."

"Got it in one, big guy. You're right. It's sucking up everything around it. And it's growing. We need to figure out how to stop it."

"How do you know?"

"That it's growing? I've been down here three times—three resets—and every time, even though everything else is the same, the hole is a little bigger. A little stronger in what it picks up. What happens if it starts to vacuum up everything around it, like trees and people?"

"Maybe it's not the worst thing."

"Excuse me?"

"Anything you find really annoying, you could toss right in this intergalactic garbage disposal, or whatever it is. People who litter, chihuahuas, televangelists—we could get rid of them in seconds, no mess."

"I had no idea you have a sense of humor."

I pause, reaching deep into my senses. I can't hear anything from the hole aside from the whisper-suck of air. What lies beyond it? An infinite void? A universe only slightly different from this one? "You need one to kill as many people as I have," I tell her.

She shudders. "Let's go back. I have something else to show you."

CHAPTER 9

BEFORE WE CLIMB back into her truck, I pause with my hand on the door handle and listen to the forest again. Nothing, not even insects chirping in the underbrush. I wonder what danger is headed our way, intent on wiping us out yet again. *As if you're a virus.* I never asked for any of this, of course—or did I?

"Too quiet," Natalie says.

I nod.

Natalie rips her door open, jumps in, and starts the engine. "Let's go," she almost shouts through the window. "I'm sensing something really bad."

She doesn't need to tell me twice—I'm plugged into the same terrible vibration, my heartbeat accelerating, my pulse loud as a dive-bombing mosquito in my ears. As I climb into the front passenger seat and buckle my seatbelt, she almost stands on the gas, skewing us onto the road. With one hand on the wheel, she draws the .45 from her holster and places it on the console between the seats.

"This other thing I wanted to show you, it's another sign something's wrong with reality . . . "

"I don't think we need more proof of that."

"You know what I mean. It's like the hole." She buckles her seatbelt, clinching it tight against her chest.

"Tell me what it is."

"Later. Let's just drive for a bit, high speed, okay? If we're too slow, something could nail us." The truck shivers as it accelerates past sixty, seventy, eighty. Good thing the road's curves have given way to a long straightaway.

My fear grows like our speed, intense but oddly exhilarating. When was the last time I was truly scared of anything? It must have been that little girl however many cycles ago, the one who could make all two hundred-odd pounds of me levitate into the air with a flick of her wrist. When I first encountered her in the camp, I made the mistake of assuming she was just another towheaded camper, easy prey in an oversized t-shirt, until she locked me with her merciless gaze. At the very end, after she'd torn off a few of my limbs, she made my prized machete fly like a guided missile, skewering me through the head before I plunged into the lake's cold waters . . .

I swallow hard. Turning my head as subtly as possible, I scan the pickup for any weapons I can use, but Natalie doesn't strike me as the kind of person to leave a chainsaw or an oversized axe in her back seat.

I'm not subtle enough. "Looking for something?" Natalie asks.

"Nothing," I say.

"Liar." She offers a shaky grin. "You want a weapon? Can't you just pop off someone's head like a cork?"

"I don't need a weapon," I say, settling back. "I'm fine."

She glances at my lap, and I look down to see my hands squeezed into hard fists, the veins throbbing. I unclench and waggle my fingers. I keep thinking about that little girl who tore me apart with just the power of her mind. What if you encounter her again? What hope do you have?

Natalie leans forward, squinting through the windshield. "What the hell is that?"

Uh-oh.

The headlights frame a pale wisp of a child maybe two hundred yards ahead. At our speed, it only takes a few seconds to close the distance, the shape resolving into a mass of long blonde hair, a white t-shirt, a pair of small, bare feet straddling the yellow line—

It's the little girl.

Natalie brakes, the truck slowing to fifty, forty, thirty miles an hour. The girl raises her head, her black eyes reflecting the headlines, her small mouth twisting into a faint smirk.

"Hit her," I wheeze through a tightening throat. "Hit her."

"What? I'm not killing a kid." Natalie shakes her head, edging the truck onto the right shoulder.

"It's not a regular kid. It'll kill us." I grip the wheel and twist it left, aiming straight at the homicidal moppet, who lifts her hands toward us, palms out and fingers splayed. She seems unconcerned about the two tons of metal bearing down on her, and why not? The last time I checked, she could bend a car into a pretzel.

Natalie keeps her left hand on the wheel, struggling against my strength, as she straight-arms her right fist into my neck. She has enough strength to make it hurt. "Whatever this is, you can't," she says, her panic sharp. "You hear me? You promised no killing."

My grip loosens on the wheel. Never mind that we're probably going to die in the next few seconds. I might be a mass-murdering creature, but I like to think of myself as a mass-murdering creature who keeps his word. And besides, we'll just come back, right?

The wheel skids through my palm, snapping me from my thoughts. "What are you doing?" I ask.

"Nothing." Natalie raises her hands. "I'm not touching anything."

The girl is controlling the wheel. The truck skews farther right, its tires rumbling off the shoulder and onto the dirt. In another moment we'll hit the ditch and flip, and if we're lucky we'll die on impact. I grip the wheel and push to the left as hard as I can, fighting what feels like a cosmic force, and the truck inches back onto the shoulder, roaring past the girl. Natalie slaps her hands on the wheel, pulling with me, but even with our combined force we barely manage to wrestle the truck into our original lane.

I glance in the rearview mirror, which frames the girl walking after us, her arms still raised, her shirt and hair crimson in the reflected glow of our taillights.

"The fuck is going on?" Natalie grunts through clenched teeth.

"She's got powers. I don't think she's human." My forearms tremble with the effort of keeping the wheel straight. How long can we keep this up? The forest falls away, the highway swooping toward the sodium glow of a gas station maybe a mile distant, a trailer park beside it. If we abandon the truck and run in there, we might buy a little time to figure something out.

"How many of you freaks are out here?" Natalie asks, and I'm about to question her use of the term 'freak' when the wheel jerks in our hands. The back of the truck rises higher and higher, the engine's roar rising to a shrill scream. The headlights flash off dark pavement filling the windshield as we flip into a stomach-destroying somersault, Natalie gripping my arms. At least we're dead, I think. At least we're dead, we're dead, we're dead—

CHAPTER 10

EXCEPT WE'RE NOT that lucky.

The truck crunches into its roof, which fails to crumple or implode. Those engineers in Detroit must know their stuff. We're dangling upside-down, tangled in our seatbelts. "I'm stuck," Natalie says, stabbing her thumbs into the seatbelt's release button.

I smell gasoline. My face hurts, and as I skim my fingers over it, I realize I never removed the Phantom of the Opera mask, which has shattered into a hundred pieces. Based on the pain, the impact shoved at least five of the larger shards into the flesh of my face. There goes my modeling career.

"Hold on," I tell Natalie, and try to unlock my seatbelt. It's jammed. I grip the buckle and pull with all my strength, tearing it from the mounting, and tumble against the dashboard. Ow. As I rise to my knees, I'm seized by an overpowering wave of nausea. Leaning through the shattered windshield, I vomit a gallon of half-digested barbecue, lake weeds and shiny .45-caliber casings onto the pavement.

"Good God," Natalie moans.

"It's okay." I wipe my mouth. "That happens a lot."

"Are those . . . bullet casings?"

"Yes. Hold on, I'm going to pull you free." I'm certain the girl is walking toward us down the highway. If we don't get out of here in the next few minutes, she's going to pull us apart like taffy.

After watching my misadventure, Natalie braces her feet against the steering wheel and presses her spine deep into her chair. I pop her seatbelt loose, and she lowers herself with more grace than you'd expect from someone who just survived a car crash. I help her through the shattered windshield, and she rises on shaky legs, carefully brushing bits of glass from her hair.

"How much time do we have?" she asks, glancing down the highway behind us.

A gnarled branch rockets from the darkness, missing my head by inches.

"None," I say.

"Hold on," she says, kneeling on the pavement. "My gun's still in the car somewhere . . . "

"No time." Grabbing her hand, I gallop for the gas station, pulling her behind me. Another branch snaps past, splintering on the pavement to our right and I steer us left, hoping to keep the wreck between us and the kid. What will happen when she starts tossing engine parts at us?

We're close enough to the gas station to see through its front windows. A bored teenager sits behind the register flipping through a magazine, a pair of headphones clamped over his ears. In the snack aisle, a thick trucker-looking dude in a blue baseball cap and grease-stained flannels considers which brand of chips will better clog his arteries. Just another ordinary night we're about to ruin.

Something black and heavy sails over our heads, banging off the gas pumps' awning, as we hit the door hard enough to almost tear it off the hinges. The teenager behind the counter gawping at us as he tears off his headphones, his right hand already reaching for the phone beside the register. For once, I'm totally fine with someone calling 911, but how much can the cops do against a girl with telekinesis and a bad temper?

"You have a back door?" Natalie snaps at him.

The teenager stares at me, his lower lip trembling, the phone loose in his hand.

"Look at me," Natalie says, louder. "You got a back door?"

The teenager nods. From the snack aisle, the trucker regards us with the wary eyes of someone who's seen everything life has to offer, only a small percentage of it good.

"Then you need to use it. Right now." Natalie shifts her gaze to the trucker. "You too."

"I don't got to do shit," the trucker rumbles. "Who's that freak with yo—"

The station's front windows pop, the glass crazing. The teenager yelps as he ducks low, sprinting from behind the counter and down the nearest aisle. The trucker on his heels, a jumbo bag of chips beneath his arm. I'm tempted to follow them, but Natalie grips my elbow, leading me behind the counter.

"Whatever you're thinking, it probably won't work," I offer.

"We're buying time." She bends down and sweeps her hands along the shelf below the register, muttering: "This is the sticks, right? He must have a gun here . . . "

"It won't do any good."

"You know, for an unstoppable murder machine, you're kind of a huge pussy," she says, her hands emerging with a silver revolver. She pops open the cylinder, revealing six shiny bullets, before snapping it closed again.

A dim shape beyond the pumps: the girl standing in the middle of the road, her arms rising slowly, her face hidden behind a curtain of shimmering hair. The air around us thrums, molecules bouncing around in panic. The ceiling rattles, shaking the fluorescents.

"Now get ready to run," Natalie says, pointing the pistol at the window and squeezing the trigger six times. A geyser of sparks from the top of the nearest pump, followed by a high-pitched whistle, and I know what's coming, my hand wraps around Natalie's collar as I drag her to the floor—

White light, searing heat, followed by a sledgehammer to the eardrums.

I'm on top of Natalie, pressing her into the tile as my back explodes in pain, scorching-hot bits of metal and glass and plastic embedded in my skin. Natalie's hands on my chest, warm and soft, reminding me of—what? Flashes of a humid night, a woman's lips brushing my ear, the faint snort of horses in the distance. Whatever it's a memory or a dream, I have no time to ruminate on it as I ramble over Natalie, pulling her through a smoky chaos of ing snack food bags.

As we reach the back door, I glance over my shoulder at the inferno beyond the windows. A tornado of fire where the pumps once stood. The girl nowhere in sight. Did we kill her? I feel an unexpected pang of sadness. Sure, the tyke tore me apart, but I always sensed she was driven by her brokenness, like a dog beaten until it only knows how to bite. Natalie's hand in mine, dragging me into the fresh air.

The rear of the gas station features a battered dumpster overflowing with garbage bags. Beside it squats a shit-brown Toyota with rusted rims and a fake tiger tail dangling from the antenna. I bet it belonged to the teenager, who's nowhere in sight. I peek through the car's side window, hoping against hope for keys in the ignition. Nothing.

"Come on," Natalie says. "Not sure how much time that fire buys us . . . "

The trucker is nowhere in sight, either. What vehicle did he come in? In the fifty seconds it took Natalie to find the gun and blow up the pumps, did he somehow manage to drive away, taking the teenager with him? If so, I wished them well.

"Woods," I say, pulling us toward the trees beyond the dumpster. Once we're far enough away, we can find another car and Natalie can take me to whatever freaked her out more than the hole torn in the universe. And when the universe finally manages to vaporize us, we'll have a little more information to work with—

A whoosh, followed by a fiery comet smashing into the gravel ten yards to our left. It's one of the pumps, reduced to a pile of melting aluminum and rubber, its heat baking our skin. Its fierce glow illuminates the girl coming around the corner of the station, her arms still outstretched, her hair swept back to reveal eyes as black and merciless as the bottom of the ocean.

"I'll find you," I tell Natalie, because we only have a second or two before we're torn into dog food.

And then something amazing happens.

A snap from the woods, followed by a buzzing like a large bee. The girl clutches her hands to her neck, weaves, and falls facedown without a sound.

I barely have time to celebrate this unexpected development before there's another snap. A sharp pain in my throat. My fingers tingle as I reach for it, feeling plastic fins, a cold metal shaft. A dart loaded with something exotic that rampages through my nervous system like a rhino, shutting down everything in its path. My muscles turn to water, and as I collapse to my knees, I see Natalie clawing at her own neck, her gaze already hazy.

From the woods emerges a line of men dressed in black fatigues and body armor and gas masks. My old friends from that mysterious facility on the far side of the lake, I assume, but the world fades away before I can ask a question or crack a chump's skull.

CHAPTER 11

I OPEN MY EYES.

I'm not on the bottom of the lake, at least.

No moon overhead, no surprised fish swimming by my feet.

Instead, I'm in a white nowhere, like the inside of a cloud.

Is this Heaven?

No, of course not. If there's an afterlife (and given all I've witnessed, I'm betting there's something after we shuffle off this mortal coil), it's a hundred percent certainty the eternal accountant overseeing the ledgers will set me up beside the furnace in Hell. Plus, Heaven wouldn't smell like disinfectant and warm plastic.

My body tingles back to life. I'm sitting on something hard. My arms and legs bound by something that feels like rope. My still-frozen neck muscles prevent me from looking down, but it feels like I'm bound to a chair or a bench of some sort.

"You awake?" It's Natalie somewhere to my right.

"Yeah," I say. "Where are we?"

"No idea," she says. "But man, I got the world's worst hangover."

My neck tingles, movement returning enough for me to tilt my head down slightly, verifying my assumption. Huge, blue bands wrap my chest and thighs, holding me to a chair as white as the surroundings. If we're in a room, it's impossible to see the seams of floor and walls.

"You never encountered anything like this?" she asks.

"No," I say. "Where's the kid?"

She chuckles. "Not here, at least."

"Thank God."

A faint hiss, and the outline of a door appears in front of us. It opens, and a stocky man steps through. He has a thick belly and scrubby beard. His gaze is cold as he crosses his meaty arms over his chest. He's dressed in a flannel shirt, unbuttoned to expose a t-shirt beneath, and a pair of ratty jeans.

"What is this?" Natalie asks. "The world's weirdest lumberjack convention?"

"That's a lame retort," the man snorts. "My name is August Jones." Pauses like that means something. Behind him, the door wheezes shut, the seams disappearing.

After a few seconds of odd silence, I ask, "And?"

August cocks an eyebrow. "There are rooms where that means something."

"And where would *those* rooms be?" Natalie laughs, but I can sense the fear in her voice. "And what kind of room is this, by the way?"

I can tilt my head enough to catch her at the edge of my vision, bound to a chair like mine. Her cheeks pale, her forehead slick with sweat. Whatever drug they used to knock us out, maybe her body isn't reacting to it well. The idea sends a jolt of fear through me. It's been many, many nights since I cared about anyone.

August raps his knuckles against the nearest portion of wall. "Kind of a Faraday cage. Blocks electromagnetic fields, but that's just the baseline. We designed it to block stable magnetic fields, as well. Which is useful if the two of you do anything . . . unexpected."

"Unexpected?" I ask. "How unexpected can we get, bound like this?"

"You're an odd-looking fellow," August says, tilting his head as he squints. "We've heard rumors of you, of course—all the drunks in town talk about the Lake Man, or whatever. I just didn't think you were real."

"I'm as real as your dreams," I say, flashing my fangs. My face might have sent hundreds of campers and townspeople into screaming shock but August seems nonplussed by it.

"My dreams always become real," he says. "The good ones, anyway."

"Where's the girl we came with?" Natalie asks. "The one who can control stuff with her mind?"

"She's the property of this facility," he says, his tone

sharpening. "And she's perfectly safe. You don't need to worry yourself about her."

"Property," Natalie says.

"Bred in a tube. The biological division of my company is a real earner. We can debate the philosophy of personhood at another time." He leans toward me. "Have we met before?"

I feel an unexpected twinge of sympathy for that kid who tried to kill us. We can't always resist our nature. I clench the muscles in my arms, hard, to see if the bands will give me a little slack. Maybe I can slide free. But the more effort I expend, the more the rubber tightens.

"Never inside here?" A slight grin tugs at the edges of August's lips.

"No." I skim my fingers along the back of the chair. It feels like metal but I lack the leverage to snap off a piece.

"But you've been around here. On another version of this very night, in fact." August's grin spreads, revealing expensive teeth. "My heads of security wanted to end you both as soon as they saw you on the road—eliminate all witnesses—but I stood them down and told them to just hit you with the drugs. You're welcome, by the way. You both seemed too interesting to kill, too much of an anomaly. When we brought you in, we took a tissue sample, ran some tests. All your little cells quantum-phasing like motherfuckers."

"I keep living this same night over and over again," I say. There's no point in lying to this man. Every bit of information will help me on the next loop.

August chuckles. "Wonderful. I love being right. We're going to get so many papers out of you, once we run our tests."

What's worse than spending eternity in the woods, killing and being killed? How about an eternity as a lab rat, subjected to endless science experiments?

"What the fuck is this place?" Natalie asks.

"Glad you asked." August pivots on his heel and raps on the wall. The whiteness fades away, like a fogbank dissolving in dawn's first light, becoming a window. Beyond the glass, row upon row of wire cages stretch out of sight, each filled with electronics, glowing red lights, forests of multicolored wires. Workers in white lab coats bustle from cage to cage, tools and clipboards in their hands.

"In simplest terms, it's a quantum computer," August says.

"We originally created it for mundane tasks, like predicting stock market movements, cracking codes, simulating thermonuclear explosions without actually setting off a bomb. That's what mundane people will pay for. They don't think big, but they often have lots of money. Once it was constructed, of course, I could adapt it surreptitiously for . . . other purposes."

As he babbles, I look around. The other walls and ceiling have become transparent. We're in a glass cube positioned maybe forty feet above this sea of cages and electronics, below a dome of rough rock so vast its crown disappears into darkness. We're far underground, maybe an abandoned mine.

"You sure love to talk," Natalie says.

"Yes." August's smile fades. "Yes, I do it quite frequently. My most recent speech was a keynote at the world's most prominent tech conference. I'd say the name of it, but it'd mean nothing to either of you. It was two hours long, more than an hour over schedule and I had them on their feet by the end, everyone applauding. I sold them on the vision of a beautiful future."

Natalie laughs and shakes her head. "I've dated a lot of guys like you."

"Smart?"

"Compensating."

August's gaze hardens. "You can try to goad me, but it won't work."

"You sure about that?" she asks.

"Anyway, moving along." August turns away, pointing at the nearest cage, which a worker has opened to adjust some wiring. "And this is where I tend to lose people with small minds. Computers are binary. The information on them is represented by bits, which are ones or zeros. But quantum computing relies on quantum bits, which can exist in a state between one and zero until they're measured, at which point they manifest as one or the other. What this means is . . . "

"Wait, I have a question," I ask.

August blasts air through his nose. "What?"

"What's a computer?" I know the answer, of course: during my education in the cabin, I read more than enough about the Antikythera mechanism, the differential analyzer, Charles Babbage's dream of a mechanical computing machine, Alan Turing, and programming.

"I don't have time for this shit," August hisses. "Listen, the point is that we have a view into multiple timelines, parallel universes. Every move you make, it births a hundred different futures, a thousand. Something impossible to calculate with a traditional computer. With this baby, though, we can see all possibilities."

"I also have a question," Natalie says.

"Is it another stupid joke?" August asks.

"No, I'm serious. This computer, it just shows you possibilities, right, nothing else? It doesn't affect reality?"

"That's how the computer was built, yes. But clearly something else is going on here." August shrugs. "Why else would you be looping?"

"You tell us," I say. "You're the brainiac."

August rubs his chin. For a moment he seems unsure of himself. "That's the thing," he almost whispers. "That's the thing."

"Wow," I say. "You have no idea. You built this huge machine and you don't have a clue why it works or what it's actually doing."

"How do you live with that face?" August stops the chin-rubbing long enough to jab a finger at me.

"Never for very long," I say. "You're avoiding the question."

"We have hypotheses. When you get down to the atomic level, matter is really nothing more than information. If there's a bug in the computer's programming, it could impact the multiverse in ways we haven't fully accounted for . . . "

"What happens if you restart it?" Natalie asks. "Or reboot it, whatever."

"We have some theories . . . "

"He doesn't know," I say.

August shakes his head. "I'm not saying that."

"You don't have to. I can see it in your eyes."

"We're going to figure it out, okay? That's science."

"That's bullshit, is more like it," Natalie says.

I've scanned the cave a few times, but I can't see any of those heavily armed guards. At least a few might lurk nearby: August, genius, wouldn't walk into a room with a pissed-off FBI agent and a murderous creature without a lot of firepower a few seconds away.

"It's not bullshit," August says, cheeks reddening, angrier than ever. "There's the very slight chance that a reboot could have catastrophic effects on—"

"It's already having catastrophic effects," Natalie says, her voice rising. "There's a hole in the sky just outside of town. It's vacuuming up everything around it, okay? And it's growing bigger."

August raises a hand for silence, his breath whistling through his nose.

Natalie almost shouts: "That's not even the worst part. I found a deer by the side of the road, but it was sort of *combined* with a tree trunk. It was still alive. I think your little science experiment here is scrambling reality all over the place, and unless we shut it off—like, right now—you're going to destroy this planet. Can your *tiny dick comprehend that*?"

"We know about the hole," August hisses.

Natalie's head jerks back. "What?"

"We know about it. We're observing it, okay? My scientists and I, we're practically living in this facility full time. And yes, we know it's growing bigger, but we have it totally under control, it's not growing at a fast enough rate to give us any real concern . . . "

I shake my head, laughter boiling up my throat.

"What's so fucking funny?" August asks. "Why the fuck are you laughing?"

I take a deep breath and hold it until the laughter dies. "I used to think I was the scariest thing around this lake," I say. "But you're way scarier, because you're oblivious. Gleefully oblivious."

August, redder than ever, a vein ticking on his forehead, grinding his teeth hard enough to break a molar as he growls, "Do you know where I went to school? How much I'm worth? The awards I've won? Because . . . "

Natalie laughing now, pressing forward against her bonds. "Fucking *men*," she says between gasps. "Why don't you whip it out . . . and mark a fence post?"

I know what we need to do. I look at her until I catch her eye. I wink. She stops laughing and her eyes widen. I hope she approves, that she's not cooking up some master plan of her own, but I don't have time to ask.

"Meet me at the camp," I tell her, and stand up. Or try to, at least. With my legs bound, I can only lift the chair maybe six inches off the ground, as I tilt forward in a weird hunch. Well, it'll do. Endless cycles of murder have given me a butcher's sense of a body's weak points. August bellows in rage as I launch myself at the wall, angling my head to the side, so when I hit that thick glass my neck br—

CHAPTER 12

BLACKNESS. THEN:

Lake bottom.

No bright moon overhead, though. Odd.

As I kick toward the surface, I think over everything August said. The man's a billionaire genius who built a quantum computer that's somehow scrambling reality like an egg. He said that turning off the computer might have catastrophic effects, but is that true? Or was he speaking from ego, unwilling to admit he might have been wrong about a few things?

A fish snaps past my face, gone in the murk, and I wonder: If we turn off the computer, will I snap out of existence? Will I break free of the loop? Or will something even weirder happen?

Whatever happens, I'm fine with it. Only so many times you can stalk through a summer camp or slaughter a diner full of rednecks. I assume Natalie will be fine with the consequences, so long as we stop that little hole in the sky from vacuuming up reality.

I break the surface, spitting water. And I see why the moon is gone.

The black hole is directly overhead. From directly beneath it, I can't measure its width, but it blocks out a huge swath of stars. The water around me ripples and jumps. I catch faint, pale flickers around the hole's edges—branches and leaves rocketing like bullets into the big nowhere.

Okay, so this is a problem.

I paddle for shore as fast as I can, pushing against the tug from above. When I reach the dock, I can't hear anything from Suzie or Trevor. They might not even be there, which would be a first. But who wants to make out beneath the apocalypse? I scramble up the piling—and see them.

Suzie and Trevor are on the dock. Actually, that's not wholly accurate: they're *in* the dock, their torsos and legs and arms melded with the warped boards, their faces frozen in agonized snarls. I wipe my left hand on my overalls and touch Suzie's cold wrist. Dead for hours.

I retrieve the rusty machete, my old friend, from the far end of the dock before marching inland. Whatever happens tonight, I hope we can reset things. Suzie and Trevor deserve to swap spit without risking a messy death.

I reach the dirt road beyond the camp's entrance. Headlights split the darkness to my left, followed by an engine's roar. A jeep pulls alongside me, the passenger door popping open to reveal Natalie behind the wheel. "You see it?" she asks.

"The hole? You can't miss it."

"It's growing really fast," she says. "Get in."

"We have to destroy that computer," I say, climbing into the passenger seat. I slip the machete into the footwell, keeping one hand on the grip. Not because I intend on using it—not now, at least—but because it's comforting. It probably won't do much good against the forces bringing about the end of the world, though.

"You think that'll stop it?"

"I hope so," I say. "But I don't know what else to do."

"And that's if we can even get close." Natalie pounds the steering wheel with the flat of her hand. "Because I have no idea how we're going to charge our way into that facility and stop that damn computer. August has a whole army."

"I actually have an idea about getting in," I say. "But I have no idea if it's incredibly brilliant or incredibly stupid. Drive to the highway."

"And then?"

"You know Joe Bubba Leonard, right? You got that land mine from him? I bet he's got a lot more explosives where that came from."

"He's also certifiably insane. And has incredibly bad taste in movies. Then again, it's not like we have a ton of options," she says, shifting into drive and easing on the gas.

We rumble down the road for another mile before I ask, "What happened after I broke my neck?"

"August tried asking me more questions, but I told him to go screw himself. I also questioned his manhood again, which is the best way to drive pretty much any man into incoherent rage. Once I suggested his giant science experiment was trying to make up for a tiny dick, he strangled me."

"Ouch."

"Whenever I pop back up," she says, "I'm in my hotel room. In the lobby, there's a table with a bunch of magazines on it. I'm running out to meet you and right there, the top magazine has August's face on it. He's the CEO of Maxim Electronics. They build computer equipment, they have big defense and healthcare contracts, they're into bioscience . . . "

"If you can call it that," I say.

"He's one of the richest men in the world, which might not mean squat in a couple of hours." She twists the wheel, bumping us onto the highway. "My gun's in the glove compartment. Want to get it out, put it on the console between us?"

I follow orders. We drive maybe another mile before our headlights flicker off a pair of distinctive rhinestone boots in the middle of the road. Joe Bubba Leonard's standing there with his rifle slung over his shoulder, his hands loose at his sides. Natalie flashes her lights and veers onto the shoulder.

"Okay," Natalie says, shifting the jeep into park and grabbing the gun. She checks the rearview mirror and opens her door and steps out, keeping her hand with the pistol below the level of the window. Joe Bubba Leonard trots onto the shoulder, squinting in confusion. It's a wonder he hasn't opened fire yet, but Natalie's presence must have short circuited his brain.

"My name is Joe Bubba Leonard," my favorite cowboy announces. "Ma'am, do you realize you're giving a ride to the most hellish abomination in at least five hundred miles?"

"I absolutely do," Natalie burbles, perkier than a cheerleader on a mountain of cocaine. "And I have a gosh-darn good reason for it."

Joe Bubba Leonard's jaw flops open but he makes no move to unsling that rifle from behind his back. "Ma'am, I hate to be contrary, but he's a damn dangerous creature . . . "

"Yes. Yes, he is," she says. "But not to me. And most definitely not to you. He's helping me save the world."

"Save the world?"

"You notice that giant hole over the lake? The one sucking up a bunch of stuff?" Natalie's hand flexes on the pistol. Despite her cheerful tone, the buzzing tension in her eyes says she'll plug the guy if he twitches wrong.

"The hole?" Joe Bubba Leonard's eyebrows shoot up. "You mean that's real?"

"It's absolutely real and it's absolutely dangerous." She downshifts her voice to its normal range. "My name's Natalie and I'm an FBI agent. This gentleman in the car with me is helping me."

"Well, I'll be." Joe Bubba Leonard snorts. "See, I thought that hole was a hallucination. Back in college, I snarfed a whole lotta whatcha might call 'questionable substances.' I even licked me a jungle frog durin' a Dario Argento screenin', which—lemme tell ya—is something I heartily do *not* recommend on a full stomach, and . . . "

"We don't have time for this," she says, reaching into her hip pocket with her free hand and pulling out a billfold, which she flicks open to reveal a shiny badge. "We need your help. You have an arsenal nearby, right?"

"FBI." Joe Bubba Leonard cracks his knuckles. "What makes me think you're not after m'guns? I know what you people do."

"You're thinking of the ATF," she says. "I just want to make sure that hole doesn't eat reality, okay? Which means we need guns."

Natalie's not persuading this guy fast enough. I open my door and climb out, wondering what'll happen if he aims that rifle and puts a bullet through my noggin before Natalie can drop him. Given how fast the hole expanded between my last go-round and the current one, this is likely our last chance.

"Look," I say. "I know you're a monster killer. I know you've killed so many monsters, you have the pelts all over the walls of your drive-in or whatever you run . . . "

"How the hell y'know that?" Joe Bubba Leonard yelps. "You readin' my mind, devil?"

"It doesn't matter," I tell him, raising a hand. "I'm sure you're the best monster killer. But there won't be any monsters to kill if we don't get this done right now. And to get it done, we need guns. Lots of guns."

"Huh." His boots creak as he sways back and forth, left and right. His brain doing its best to crunch through a lot of weird data. As we wait for him to finish those calculations, a truck roars past—the same one that splattered him in my previous loop.

"Okay," he says. "You made some darn good points. But if I do this, I don't wanna pay taxes no more."

"I'll see what I can do," Natalie says, struggling to keep a straight face.

"Okay. I'm parked up a'ways." He turns away from us and trots down the shoulder, disappearing into the dark beyond our headlights.

"Well, that seems to have worked," Natalie says as she climbs back into the jeep and shifts into drive. "What's your next brilliant idea?"

"You're going to hate it," I tell her.

CHAPTER 13

AS IT TURNS OUT, Joe Bubba Leonard has his arsenal in two duffel bags in the high weeds beside the road, which is why I didn't find it when I took his car. He unzips both, revealing enough armaments to give any gun nut a serious woodie: pistols, shotguns, rifles, even a crossbow.

"Take any of 'em," he says, pulling out a stubby gun with a fat barrel. "But here's mine. His name's Thumper."

"What's Thumper do?" I ask.

"Launches a pretty little grenade."

"I'm fine with this," I say, hefting the machete.

"How many explosives you got?" Natalie asks.

It's like asking Santa whether he has enough flying reindeer for Christmas night. With a high-wattage grin, Joe Bubba Leonard kneels and sorts through the bag until he finds not only the land mine that once turned me into a blood-mist, but also several bundles of dynamite.

I hope it's enough. Thirty minutes later, I sit in the woods alone, the machete across my knees. I left Natalie and Joe Bubba Leonard on the road loading those explosives into the jeep. When the time comes, Natalie will set a heavy stone on the jeep's gas pedal, sending the vehicle on a magical journey into the front gate of August's massive complex. The rest of the plan hinges on a lot of luck, but it's not like we have good alternatives.

The trees moan and rustle. I can't feel any wind. I wonder if the hole over the lake is large enough to create its own weather system, sucking up the atmosphere like a sugared-up kid with a straw and a can of soda. Beyond the pines, I have a good angle on the fence lining the facility, and beyond it the enormous flank of a building. The fence hums with thousands of volts.

A distant roaring from the road grows louder.

I stand, flexing my grip on the blade.

From a couple hundred yards away, the jeep colliding with the heavily armored gate sounds like two metal plates slapping together. The fence vibrates and crackles, the hum cutting off. A fireball rises above the trees, spewing greasy smoke.

I run for the fence, wrap my fingers through the chain link, and climb as fast as I can. A rising crackle of gunfire from the road. I'm frightened for Natalie, but I figure the best way to help her is to shut down August's machine as fast as I can. Kill the power, blow up that whole floor of cages and machinery, whatever it takes.

I leap from the fence and sprint across the grass, expecting a line of guards to emerge from the darkness. To my left, the gunfire intensifies, punctuated by a hollow boom—Joe Bubba Leonard deploying Thumper, I bet. To my right, the facility's unbroken expanse of gray is broken by a grid of blue scaffolding covered in clear tarps. Construction. I angle toward it, hoping it's a weak spot, hoping there are no guards or cameras.

I punch through a tarp into the interior.

It's raw space in here, three stories' worth of scaffolding extending into the distance, illuminated by strings of lights in cages.

It's also filled with men in black body armor and masks, most of them crouching behind barrels or stacks of lumber, all of them armed with rifles bristling with scopes and extra-long ammunition clips.

Either the assault on the front gate has failed to draw most of the facility's guards, or August filled this building with every rent-a-cop and mercenary between here and Alaska. Bulky guys, the kind who live on steroids and cocaine and raw meat.

I look down at my chest lit by a hundred red laser-dots.

"Oh shi—" I say, on reflex, before a hundred fingers squeeze a hundred triggers, and the construction site explodes in a hurricane of supersonic lead. I leap toward a solid-looking block of marble, but my supernatural reflexes aren't quite fast enough to spare me from damage. An explosion inside my shoulder, a blinding flash of light behind my eyes, and I'm behind the marble but my right arm is a shredded mess, butchered nerves and tendons shrieking in anguish.

At least the damage wasn't worse. Bullets chew through stacks of drywood and bags of cement, filling the air with a pale fog. Visibility zero. When I try to lift my right arm, nothing happens, not even a twitching finger. I tear a strip from my overalls and wrap it around my arm just below the shoulder, tightening it beyond the point of agony, but at least the mangled limb stops bleeding.

Footsteps crunching on the gritty floor. With my rough torniquet cinched, I scoop up a chunk of broken marble and, rising to my knees, throw it in that direction as hard as I can. A thud, followed by a gurgling scream and the echoing crash of a body hitting the floor. On the scaffolding, someone fires off a burst, bullets stitching the floor to my right.

I risk a peek around the marble barrier. A guard slumps against the far side, his cracked helmet oozing blood. I grip the edge of his bullet-resistant vest and begin to pull him toward me as another gunshot plows into his back. I retreat, wondering how long it will take for all these men to find their bravery and swarm me. Our best hope is for Natalie and Joe Bubba Leonard to punch through the gate and shut down the computer, but do they have the firepower to make that happen? A sinking sensation in my gut says no.

A click from overhead.

"Stop firing, you idiots," August says, his voice amplified by enormous speakers.

To my right, someone curses in surprise.

"Lake Man," August says. "You there?"

I give him nothing.

"I hate to admit this," August chuckles. "But I might have been wrong about this whole situation. I've been reviewing the computer's records. All the possible permutations of tonight. You've been through a lot, haven't you? Coming back again and again and again, always at the bottom of that lake. You and I even met once, after we captured you."

The fog dissipates as all those particles drift back to the floor. I have only a minute or two. No chunks of marble or other weapons in sight, except for a hardwood moving dolly just beyond my reach. Its little wheels give me an idea. I lean toward it, my hands outstretched.

"You might be wondering about your origins," August says. "Where you came from. Why you're so hard to kill."

I freeze.

"Well, I don't have a definitive answer for you," he continues. "But I have some pretty smart scientists underground here, and they think you came from nothing. What we've discovered, with quantum theory, is that particles just sort of . . . appear. Things can manifest into existence without any reason or cause, all without violating the laws of physics. My scientists, they think you just appeared in that lake, already stuck in the loop from the first moment you opened your eyes. No past, no family. I know that sounds terrible, but isn't it sort of a relief?"

"No," I mutter, reaching around the marble for the dead guard. I tug him close enough to pluck the other item I need from his belt.

"You're a cosmic anomaly," August booms, so loud it quakes the particles drifting past my face. "No reason for your existence. But you're strong, and fast, and have no compunction whatsoever about killing. I could use someone with your skills and I can pay whatever price you want. Your friends outside, we'll even let them live. What do you say?"

I roll on top of the dolly, which creaks beneath my weight. Pushing with my toes, I angle it toward the ramp I spied before everything went to hell—the one that leads to the steel door. I can only hope that door opens into the facility's depths.

"What about the hole?" I yell, because I need a little more time. I place the hand grenade I took from the dead guard on the floor, pinning it in place with my mangled arm, and very carefully pull the pin with my good hand, making sure the spoon stays in place.

"What about it?" August sounds angry again, and I imagine his face flushing like it did in the glass room.

"Growing bigger."

"Yes, yes, we know. But we have an eye on it, okay? We have some plans."

"August, you're so full of bullshit, I'm surprised it's not coming out your mouth."

And with that witty *bon mot*, I snatch up the hand grenade and toss it as hard as I can down the ramp, toward the door. Men scream. One, two, three, boom. A sideways blast of steel scraps and paint chips. I'm already rolling atop the dolly, down the ramp, toward the jagged rectangle of smoky light.

In my head, it was a good plan, one that rolled me to safety fast as a rocket. In reality, guards open fire from a dozen directions before I make it more than a few yards. Hits to the leg, shoulder, and lower back—a supernova of pain. I shriek as the dolly rolls through the door and collides with a wall, spilling me onto cool linoleum.

I try to stand and my left leg buckles, dark blood seeping from a teacup-sized hole in my thigh. My impact with the wall left a significant dent. From the far end of the hallway, two lines of guards appear, their rifles raised. Yelling from the construction site as those men regroup. I'm trapped.

No.

I need as much energy as I can muster, so I unleash a bellow so loud I feel like it might shatter the lights and shake the walls. The hallway guards freeze, wavering, and a savage burst of joy courses through my veins, pure as adrenaline. That's right, guys. The monster is in your house.

Favoring my still-functional right leg, I leap at the wall, which implodes under my weight. I'm in a blank white room devoid of furniture. Still screaming, I throw myself one-legged at the next wall, crunching through it into an office, where I bounce off desks like a bloody pinball before crashing through yet another wall. I'm almost blind from dust, my mouth stuffed with drywall, my tendons aching like my limbs are about to pop off. There's something wrong with the floor now, my feet sinking into it like quicksand, making me think of Suzie and Trevor frozen in the dock. A shimmering in the air like a shockwave passing through and I'm tumbling down, down, down—

CHAPTER 14

THE DARKNESS IS ABSOLUTE. The hum and click of machinery. I lay there, spitting drywall and trying to breathe. Where am I? I can't even see any light from the hole I fell through. Maybe the impact blinded me.

"I'm a genius and I still don't understand you," August's amplified voice booms through the void. "You're nothing. You're not even a killer, because everyone you take out, they just come back. You're a quirk, a mistake of the universe or our quantum computer—basically the same thing, at this point. Why keep going? Why not just lie down and wait for us to find you?"

"I have a purpose now," I say, not caring if he hears me or not.

Except that's a lie.

I *had* a purpose, but I failed.

And trying your best doesn't quite count when existence itself is at stake.

Something buzzes past my face, and I swipe at it. The motion activates lights overhead, which click to life in sequence, revealing bits and pieces of a high-tech laboratory, the walls lined with machinery behind glass panels. The middle of the space is dominated by what looks like an operating table. Now I can see the jagged hole I fell through, stuffed with loose wiring and ductwork, a straight plunge through the bowels of the building.

I'm no August Jones when it comes to quantum physics, but I'm betting the black hole over the lake has started to warp the fabric of reality, like how an omelet in a hot skillet will bubble in different places. Particles disappear or invert or scramble, and suddenly you have a deer buried in a tree, a couple of kids inside a dock, or a monster tumbling through a floor solid as mist.

That same hum-click, and I look up as a mechanical arm unhinges from the ceiling, sliding toward me on a track. At the end of the arm is a bright red orb.

"Evaluating subject," the orb growls in a deep electronic voice.

Is this a weapon? At the very least, it might alert August and other goons to my location. I try to rise, to tear it from the track, but my throbbing, burning, tingling body refuses to move.

"Evaluation complete," the orb says. "Massive damage to biological tissue discovered. Impossible to save limbs. Advised course of action: cybernetics. Do you consent?"

"Yes?" I offer. The floor trembles, or maybe it's my nerve endings twitching as they shut down. I have nothing to lose.

"Subject consent," the orb says. "Operation begins."

From the ceiling unfurl a dozen more mechanical arms, each loaded with a different implement: needles, saws, blades, and more. One of the glass panels slides back, the machinery behind it cycling to a shrill whine, lights flashing across its control panels.

"Maybe . . . maybe this isn't a good idea," I manage to say before the clicking arms plunge into my mangled body.

CHAPTER 15

ASK ME HOW it feels to have a spider robot slice off your ruined parts and bolt on cybernetic replacements, silver and segmented like a bug's armor.

The answer: Fantastic, at least once you get past the agony of surgery. And once you get used to how your new arms and legs click and hum every time you move.

The mechanical arm with the red orb retreats into the ceiling without so much as a goodbye. I flex my new arm, hop on my new legs, bend to stretch the new spine implanted in my back. The cybernetic bits tingle like limbs waking from sleep.

A click from overhead. "Ah, there you are, you moron," August says. "Found our way to the cybernetic lab, did we? Lucky you. Or unlucky you, actually, because we can remotely control all of those enhancements through the syst—"

A loud boom, followed by a burst of crackling feedback.

"Are you there?" Natalie asks. "How do I work this fucking thing?"

"Yes," I say, searching the lab for a door, finding one to my left. It's the most armored door I've ever seen in my endless life, a monstrosity of thick steel and rivets and bolts, with a porthole in the middle too small for my fist. I peer through the porthole, but the glass is too smeared to see anything other than vague shapes, a patch of whiteness.

Just for laughs, I yank on the doorknob. Locked.

"Oh yeah, there you are. All sorts of monitors here," she says. "Listen, I just shot August. No big loss for the world, but we're pinned down here."

"Where are you?" I shout at the ceiling. Stepping back, I raise my new left foot and drive it into the doorknob, more out of frustration than anything else. A motor whirs to life beneath my knee and my metallic leg becomes a rocket, connecting with the steel hard enough to make my body thrum like a tuning fork.

Wonder of wonders, the door crumples inwards. I step back, amazed, as it tears off its hinges and tumbles to the floor with a gonglike boom.

Hey, I could get used to this.

"I'm in a control room," Natalie says. "Most of August's men fled, but there's still a bunch outside. Bubba's having a lot of fun holding them off, but he's low on ammo."

"Can you shut down the computer?"

"I don't know." An amplified thud as she smacks something. "There are too many buttons. No idea how this system works."

"Okay," I say as I duck through the doorway. "We'll figure something out."

"Better be soon," she says, her voice quaking. "The forest? I can see it from here. The branches are stripping off like a hurricane . . . "

I'm standing in a windowless metal room. At its far end, in a fierce spotlight, sits an enormous glass cube, a pile of white blankets inside. I step closer. There's something in the blankets. I spy a wisp of blonde hair, the curve of an arm.

It's the little girl, fast asleep.

I want to turn around and run. Imagine the damage she could do if her mind grips my metal parts. I spin, looking for another exit, and spy a line of tiny monitors bolted to the table to my right. Each screen displays a view of the outside world in glorious black and white.

I can see Natalie standing at a control panel, punching buttons. August lies beside her feet, a bloody hole in his chest, his dead eyes wide.

I can see Joe Bubba Leonard in a smoky corridor, his movie-star grin wide and bright as he fires a submachine gun at a swarm of guards.

I can see the perimeter fence swaying, the trees beyond it thrashing, a storm of leaves and stones and branches levitating into the void.

The fourth view is a blank corridor, maybe outside this very room. Two dozen guards line the walls, loading weapons and prepping what look like explosives. Even with my cybernetic parts, they have enough firepower to turn me into a spine in a sack.

Everything is imploding. We have maybe minutes left.

Taped to the wall beyond the monitors: A single sheet of paper with the grainy, gray image of what looks like a lump of meat. Bold text above the image proclaims: '*BEWARE! This is what test subject can do to YOU!*'

A faint cough. I turn—and freeze in fear. The girl's eyes open. She regards me with soft curiosity.

"Who are you?" she asks, her voice oddly electronic. I spot the small speaker near the top of a glass panel. The cube is too thick for sound to pass through on its own, and I wonder if that curbs her powers somehow.

"I don't have a name," I tell her. It's a funny thing to admit.

"I'm Jill," she says, sitting up. "That's the name I gave myself."

"It's a very nice name."

"Thank you." She squints, blinks, smiles. "You got a funny face."

"It is, isn't it? Some people don't like it, but it's mine, you know?"

"I like it. Would you like a name?"

"Sure."

"How about Bob?"

"Bob."

"Do you like it?"

The floor vibrates beneath my soles. For a moment, I think it's the girl using her mind, except she looks startled, like she's also felt it. The void outside is growing larger, hungrier. It could dissolve the floors and swallow us whole at any moment.

I have an idea.

"Do you want to get out of there?" I ask her.

Her eyes widen. "And go where?" she asks.

I shrug. "Anywhere."

"I've never been out of here before. Can I tell you a secret?"

"Absolutely."

"I heard a nurse talking. She said there was a place on the other side of the lake, and it had good chocolate milkshakes. I've never had a milkshake before. I would very much like a milkshake."

"Milkshakes are good."

She frowns. "I was going to go out tonight. When they came with dinner, I was going to make them let me out. I can do that now. They don't know it, though."

A muted scraping sound to my left. On the fourth monitor, the guards are taping black boxes to the wall, running wires down the hallway. They're right on the other side, ready to punch through.

"I'll take you for a milkshake," I say. "Just don't hurt me, okay?"

"Of course not." Her frown flips into the broad smile of a girl who enjoys watching cartoons and hanging out with her friends, living a normal life in a normal town. "We're friends, right?"

"Right." She was never evil, I realize. She was just scared and confused and angry, lashing out at anything and everything. Just like me.

"Hit that," she says, pointing to a big red button atop a metal plate beside the cube.

After a microsecond of hesitation, I push the button and the harsh light plays over seams in the cube's side, a small door wheezing open on clear hinges. As Jill steps outside the cube, I feel a maddening itch deep in my brain.-

"I can see inside you," she says, her fingers shaking. "It's very bad outside."

"It is," I say. "But I know what might fix it. Will you help me?"

"Yes."

I tilt my face to the ceiling. "Natalie!" I yell, hoping she can hear me. "Get Joe Bubba and get out!"

CHAPTER 16

JILL RAISES HER HANDS.

The walls tremble.

The tremble deepens into a roar so intense it almost liquifies every cell in my body.

I grip the nearest table, clenching my jaw to hold back any screaming.

Jill winks at me and curls her hands into fists.

Above us, the infinite floors of August's massive complex peel back like a concrete flower. Split wiring erupts in showers of sparks, broken pipes spit water, ductwork sprays steam. The shriek of twisting metal, or maybe it's the sound of people trapped beneath all that shifting tonnage, fills the air.

Now up, Jill says, not out loud—in my head. She lifts her left arm, fingers wide, and we're flying up, rocketing faster and faster toward the night. An echoing boom rises from beneath us. I look down at a sea of fire consuming the building's lowest levels, shrinking to a pinpoint of orange light as we burst free of the building and soar into the night.

I catch a glimpse of Natalie and Joe Bubba Leonard sprinting across a field toward the burning remains of the front gate. Nobody else in sight. If any guards or scientists survived, they're too busy fleeing for their lives to bother us.

I can see the glittering surface of the lake—glittering because the moon is full overhead, the black splotch of the hole shrinking upon itself. The silvery forests stretching into the distance, broken at points by the flickering lights of houses and towns. It's beautiful in miniature. I can only hope it's all reset down there, everyone alive and whole.

Jill shakes her head, slowing our ascent. We float on the wind like balloons.

"What will you do now?" Jill asks.

"Read," I say. There are too many books and too little time in this world. Whatever my growing feelings for Natalie, I know she'll return to her old life, leaving me alone. Maybe I can build a little cabin on the lake and fill it with a library. Maybe I can watch over Jill as she grows up. That sounds like a nice afterlife.

"Milkshake first," Jill says, smiling.

"Milkshake first."

We descend, Jill aiming at the road just beyond the complex's gate. Natalie and Joe Bubba Leonard walk to meet us. The air smells like a couple billion dollars in burning electronics.

A hundred feet above the ground, Jill asks, "Are we monsters?"

"Yes," I say. "But it's not our fault. We're creatures of circumstance."

"Are we evil?"

"You're not," I say. "I've done evil things. But you know what? I know I need to change. I'm trying to change. And that counts for something, right?"

Jill takes my hand in hers, squeezes. "I hope so."

We're about to land. Natalie and Joe Bubba Leonard are smeared in dried blood and soot and bits of debris, all of which makes their teeth seem extra-white as they smile. I'm looking forward to that cool, sweet milkshake and maybe some tangy barbecue, and if Joe Bubba Leonard tries anything weird, I'll snap his arm for old times' sake.

CHAPTER 17

I OPEN MY EYES.
Blue morning sky.
Beautiful.

THE END?

Not if you want to dive into more of Crystal Lake Publishing's Tales from the Darkest Depths!

Check out our amazing website and online store or download our latest catalog here.

We always have great new projects and content on the website to dive into, as well as a newsletter, behind the scenes options, social media platforms, our own dark fiction shared-world series and our very own webstore. If you use the IGotMyCLPBook! coupon code in the store (at the checkout), you'll get a one-time-only 50% discount on your first eBook purchase!

Our webstore even has categories specifically for KU books, non-fiction, anthologies, and of course more novels and novellas.

DARK
TIDE

ABOUT THE AUTHORS

Glenn Rolfe is an author from the haunted woods of New England. He has studied Creative Writing at Southern New Hampshire University and continues his education in the world of horror by devouring the novels of Stephen King, Richard Laymon, Brian Keene, Jack Ketchum, and many others. He has three children, Ruby, Ramona, and Axl. He is grateful to be loved despite his weirdness.

He is a Splatterpunk Award nominee and the author of *August's Eyes, Until Summer Comes Around, Blood and Rain*, and many, many more.

Tom Deady's first novel, *Haven,* won the 2016 Bram Stoker Award for Superior Achievement in a First Novel. He has since published several novels, novellas, a short story collection, and the first book in his middle grade horror series. He has a Master's Degree in English and Creative Writing and is a member of both the Horror Writers Association and the New England Horror Writers Association.

Nick Kolakowski is the author of *Love & Bullets, Boise Longpig Hunting Club, Absolute Unit,* and other novels of crime and terror. His short stories have appeared in *Dark Moon Digest, Mystery Tribune, Thuglit, Rock and a Hard Place Magazine*, and various anthologies. He lives and writes in New York City.

Readers . . .

Thank you for reading *Monsters*. We hope you enjoyed this 5th book in our Dark Tide series.

If you have a moment, please review *Monsters* at the store where you bought it.

Help other readers by telling them why you enjoyed this book. No need to write an in-depth discussion. Even a single sentence will be greatly appreciated. Reviews go a long way to helping a book sell, and is great for an author's career. It'll also help us to continue publishing quality books. You can also share a photo of yourself holding this book with the hashtag #IGotMyCLPBook!

Thank you again for taking the time to journey with Crystal Lake Publishing.

Visit our Linktree page for a list of our social media platforms.
https://linktr.ee/CrystalLakePublishing

Crystal Lake Publishing's most popular anthologies:

Our Mission Statement:

Since its founding in August 2012, Crystal Lake Publishing has quickly become one of the world's leading publishers of Dark Fiction and Horror books in print, eBook, and audio formats.

While we strive to present only the highest quality fiction and entertainment, we also endeavour to support authors along their writing journey. We offer our time and experience in non-fiction projects, as well as author mentoring and services, at competitive prices.

With several Bram Stoker Award wins and many other wins and nominations (including the HWA's Specialty Press Award), Crystal Lake Publishing puts integrity, honor, and respect at the forefront of our publishing operations.

We strive for each book and outreach program we spearhead to not only entertain and touch or comment on issues that affect our readers, but also to strengthen and support the Dark Fiction field and its authors.

Not only do we find and publish authors we believe are destined for greatness, but we strive to work with men and woman who endeavour to be decent human beings who care more for others than themselves, while still being hard working, driven, and passionate artists and storytellers.

Crystal Lake Publishing is and will always be a beacon of what passion and dedication, combined with overwhelming teamwork and respect, can accomplish. We endeavour to know each and every one of our readers, while building personal relationships with our authors, reviewers, bloggers, podcasters, bookstores, and libraries.

We will be as trustworthy, forthright, and transparent as any business can be, while also keeping most of the headaches away from our authors, since it's our job to solve the problems so they can stay in a creative mind. Which of course also means paying our authors.

We do not just publish books, we present to you worlds within your world, doors within your mind, from talented authors who sacrifice so much for a moment of your time.

There are some amazing small presses out there, and through collaboration and open forums we will continue to support other presses in the goal of helping authors and showing the world what quality small presses are capable of accomplishing. No one wins when a small press goes down, so we will always be there to support hardworking, legitimate presses and their authors. We don't see Crystal Lake as the best press out there, but we will always strive to be the best, strive to be the most interactive and grateful, and even blessed press around. No matter what happens over time, we will also take our mission very seriously while appreciating where we are and enjoying the journey.

What do we offer our authors that they can't do for themselves through self-publishing?

We are big supporters of self-publishing (especially hybrid publishing), if done with care, patience, and planning. However, not every author has the time or inclination to do market research, advertise, and set up book launch strategies. Although a lot of authors are successful in doing it all, strong small presses will always be there for the authors who just want to do what they do best: write.

What we offer is experience, industry knowledge, contacts and trust built up over years. And due to our strong brand and trusting fanbase, every Crystal Lake Publishing book comes with weight of respect. In time our fans begin to trust our judgment and will try a new author purely based on our support of said author.

With each launch we strive to fine-tune our approach, learn from our mistakes, and increase our reach. We continue to assure our authors that we're here for them and that we'll carry the weight of the launch and dealing with third parties while they focus on their strengths—be it writing, interviews, blogs, signings, etc.

We also offer several mentoring packages to authors that include knowledge and skills they can use in both traditional and self-publishing endeavours.

We look forward to launching many new careers.

This is what we believe in. What we stand for. This will be our legacy.

Welcome to Crystal Lake Publishing—
Tales from the Darkest Depths.